THE
NIGHT DANCER
CHRONICLES

BOOK ONE

ANTHONY GERO

Auburn, NY

Cover illustration by Alan Archambault.

For information on this title contact:
Downtown Books Publishing
66 Genesee Street
Auburn, NY 13021
downtownbooksandcoffee.com/

ISBN 978-0-692-32290-1

To Stan Gosek
*My good friend who, as we grew up, shared our love of
sci-fi, good horror movies, and music.*

ACKNOWLEDGEMENTS

For their grand assistance to me on this *Night Dancer* series, I wish to thank John and Mary Ann Patterson for their comments, Alan Archambault for his inspired drawing, Ryan and John at Downtown Books & Coffee for their business sense, my daughters Theresa and Kate who always encouraged me on this series, and, finally, to my greatest copy editor and tolerant wife, Linda Crye-Gero, whoa, we did it!

BOOK I

1914 – 1938

"And the Lord said to Satan, 'Have you considered my servant Job, that there is none like him on the earth, a blameless and upright man, who fears God and turns away from evil? He still holds fast his integrity, although you incited me against him to destroy him without reason.'"

—Job 2:3

"We enter parliament (i.e. The Reichstag) in order to supply ourselves, in the arsenal of democracy, with its own weapons... If democracy is so stupid as to give us free tickets and salaries for this bear's work, that is its affair... We do not come as friends, nor even as neutrals. We come as enemies. As the wolf burst into the flock, we come."

—Joseph Goebbels (1928)

"What is faith but a kind of betting or speculation after all? It should be, 'I bet that my Redeemer liveith.'"

—Samuel Butler (1815-1902)

ONE

Death's rhythm, as in birth, has its own meter, its own tempo, so as his pain came again, Brother Ivan just lay on his bed enduring his suffering like Job in the Bible. Ivan's labored breaths made it difficult for his mind to focus, but an old prayer, one taught to him before he had entered the monastery helped. "Be still and know that I am with you," he recited faithfully, but as he finished this latest recitation, a thought came to him and he cried out, "Will she come?"

Only silence answered.

While his tired eyes scanned the whitewashed walls of his cell, they finally settled on a plain wooden cross that hung at the foot of his bed. "You suffered too, Lord," Ivan mumbled, then shook his head. "So long ago," he sputtered then raised his right hand and wiped some sweat from his cheek. "Strange," he murmured as an unsettling urgency came over him, a feeling he hadn't felt for a long time. "Is it her?" he uttered as he tossed about. No, his mind raced, it's not her, not Mary for I felt no fear with her. This is something else, he concluded, then raised himself weakly up on his elbow and called out in a panic, "Who's there?"

Again, there was no answer.

As Ivan stared ahead, by the moon's pale light flittering into the room from the small window, he could just see beads of moisture on the walls as the warm air seemed to be forming into a fine mist that was beginning to materialize at the end of the bed. "Are you Death, come to take me home?" Ivan asked as the emerging shadow moved closer.

"No," a voice replied from deep within the shadow, "it is I."

"Who?"

"I," the voice hissed back

"How can that be?" Ivan screamed, his voice trembling with fear as the realization of what it was over came him. "You can't be in God's house!"

"God's house is open to all," the voice responded with a chuckle, "even for the likes of one such as me."

"Blasphemer," Ivan spat back.

"True enough, true enough, but it is time," the voice countered harshly, "so are you ready, little brother?"

"Yes," he answered resignedly, "so, like Job, I will trust in God."

"Should you, Ivanosovich?" and the shape formed into a hooded man and leaped onto the monk's bed. "Well now," it crooned, "let's see, do you know why I'm here?"

Ivan remained mute.

"Come," it said, its supple voice pitiless, its tone dripping with no remorse, "surely at the hour of your death, you can still have hope."

Ivan looked up and could see the thing's triumphant smile. Where is my courage? Ivan thought as he fought the impetus to speak and berated himself for his fear. In an old Army trick, he bit his lips hard trying to focus on that pain instead of the evil he knew he was about to face.

"Still the stoic, Ivanosovich," the figure sneered. With a sweep of its hand, it pointed towards a wall and said, "Look, little brother, behold the new millennium, the new age of 20th century man!" With that, the creature hopped off Ivan's bed and stood nearby. "See," the figure exclaimed as flickering images of people began to move like in a movie film, "the blood red dawn comes!" As Ivan felt drawn to watch, the Archduke Ferdinand was assassinated at Sarajevo after which a world war erupted, slaughtering millions in the trenches. "The three children at Fatima," the creature said calmly, "will be shown all this and more by the Lord's mother, but few will believe what the children will try to reveal. Their warnings will go unheeded by God's flock, especially since the Church hides the truth." The beast laughed wickedly at its statement. "There is nothing they, or she or you," and it turned to Ivan, "can do that will stop these events and others much greater from happening."

Ivan began to sob as the events following World War I led into World War II played upon the wall.

"God waits," the creature exclaimed, "for this new test of his people's faith and does nothing to prevent it." Just then, a great ball of fire and flames mushroomed across the white washed walls of his cell. "Our time, little brother, approaches," the hooded figure exclaimed, "and soon the world will be ours, so come, join with me," and it turned towards Ivan. "Save yourself! Renounce God in this last hour of your life and accept my Master. Come...," and the black-cloaked thing extended a hand, but Ivan shook his head and looked away. "Peasant!" The word was spat out. "What has your God done for the World? Will he avert these wars, these atrocities, these crimes?" The statements were full of mockery. "Will God stop his children's warring madness?"

Ivan moaned and closed his eyes.

"Come, little brother," the creature cooed with a siren's silkiness. "God will not save the World, nor will he save you," and paused, "but I can." Instantly, the thing sprung back on the monk's bed, shook off its cape's hood and took Ivan's head into its bony hands. "Come," it sweetly beckoned as it drew nearer, "come to me."

Ivan's eyes filled with fright at the gleaming white fangs and the vampire's blond hair falling about its shoulders. Ivan tried to speak, but his chest was rapidly filling with fluids and in a final great spasm of pain, his arms flung themselves out, his eyes opened wide, and he gasped loudly.

At this death spasm, the vampire pulled back and snorted, for like a great cat, once the thrill of a kill is over, there was no joy in playing with the dead monk now. The beast looked around, knowing that Ivan would not keep the journal there for it knew its prey from their past encounters. To spend any more time here is useless, it thought, so in a swirl of mist, it rose and flowed out through the cell's window. Once among the clouds, it reformed itself into a great bat and glided gently on the air currents like a dancer floating across a ballroom floor. On the vampire flew, back to its lair, back to its precious earth, illuminated in its journey by twinkling stars. "Soon enough, soon enough," it sang, "soon enough."

The novice was on his way to morning prayers when he stopped by to look in on his mentor, Brother Ivan. What the young man found caused him to scream so loudly that several nearby monks ran to the cell. For those who entered, the vivid horror on Ivan's face was enough to cause most to flee in terror, making the sign of the cross as they ran.

When the Abbot arrived and entered the cell, several of the older monks were there, the monastery's mortician amongst them. Ivan was, as he had been found, on the simple bed like a crucified Christ. Ivan's arms were flung wide and his eyes were fully open and staring at the ceiling. His mouth was locked in a firm gawk, while his swollen tongue flopped limp to one side. "Fold his arms," the Abbott sputtered as he made the sign of the cross over the corpse, but due to the rigor mortis, the mortician had to snap Ivan bones to do so which caused the Abbott to flinch.

Brother Nicholas, the oldest of the monks at the monastery, had finally arrived by then and as he stood next to the Abbott said, "Close the eyes."

"Yes," the Abbott murmured, "quickly now."

When that was completed, the mortician motioned to the other brothers present to come over. After they raised the corpse on their shoulders, they began to shuffle out, headed for the mortuary.

"The Devil has been in our house," Brother Nicholas mumbled as the body passed by.

"Be still," the Abbott countered harshly in a low tone.

"I will not," Nicholas snapped quickly. "It was I who befriended Ivan when he first came here, after that incident at the pass, and it was I who knew his worst fears about that vile creature."

"Yes, I know Brother Nicholas," the Abbott responded as he looked around hesitantly to make sure no other monks were lurking about. "But surely God would not allow such an evil thing in our house?"

"God could Reverend Abbott, God could."

"It is warm in here," the Abbott stated as he mopped his forehead with the palm of his hand.

Nicholas just nodded.

"Even in our house?" the Abbott asked as he leaned in closer.

"Yes,' Nicholas said softly, "even here."

Nicholas' words were a catalyst for the Abbott. "Tell no one, Nicholas, no one," to which he gave a low grunt. "Once we have buried Brother Ivan," the Abbott continued, "you and I will perform the ritual of cleansing here, Brother," and the Abbott put his hand on the old man's shoulder. "These are bad times."

"Bad times," the grizzled monk echoed, "bad."

The Abbott nodded and then left quickly.

After he had gone, Nicholas made the sign of the cross and dropped to the floor to say a brief prayer for Ivan's soul. While the old man knelt, on the still damp floor, after he finished the prayer, he grabbed hold of the bed frame, rose, and as he did, he beheld the cross on the wall. "Even here in God's house," he muttered then added, "So Ivan was right. Satan's agents are among us." As the pain in his old knees grew, Nicholas shuffled off and began to navigate his way down the hall. Will he come? Nicholas wondered and shrugged. Strange, he thought, how old men use shrugs to answer questions, and he chuckled. "Yes," Nicholas mumbled loudly, "I will not forget my duty, Ivan, but what a world, what a world," the old monk continued. "Evil everywhere." As he shook his head he could just make out the entrance to the stairs.

When Nicholas arrived at the curved stairwell that seemed to stretch below and beyond his sight, he carefully began the steep descent. With each step, the pain in his legs stabbed at him. Will he come?" he muttered, then took another step down and said, "Will he come?" Finally, at the third step, Nicholas paused as a thought came to him. He smiled, then stepped down gingerly saying, "Will he come?" and paused, again. While Nicholas peered into the darkness of that stairwell, he knew he had a long way to travel. With determination, he put his hand on the wall, put his foot out, and as he dropped down to the next step, chanted, "Will he come?"

His words echoed in the vastness of that stairwell.

He did this at each of the 39 steps before he reached the bottom. Once there, he shuffled off slowly, down the corridor, to find the monastery's gatekeeper.

TWO

Every day Brother Nicholas had held his vigil where he sat by the high window and watched and hoped, and thought, Will he come, but the man from Dublin didn't. However, on this bright day, a motion caught Nicholas attention on the path below. It first appeared to be a black dot that moved steadily towards the monastery that as the dot got closer, took on a human form. As a result, the monk rose expectantly, placing a hand over his eyebrows and peered harder. "Is it him?" he muttered. "Has he come?"

Out on the trail, the Irishman sweated profusely, for it was a steep climb, even for Captain Sean Stoker. The ascent to St. Constantine's Monastery was purposely hard and why it had been selected for its remoteness over 500 years ago. "The time of troubles," Brother Ivan had told Stoker in 1905 when he had visited his friend Ivan. "For these people, five centuries is only yesterday," and Ivan looked over at Sean, "but each day, one can see the Lord's wonders from here." Ivan pointed to several small, wispy clouds. "The old monks call them God's angels," and Ivan chuckled. "After a while here, you can see why." Today, as Stoker came back to the monastery once again, he noticed several small clouds floating gracefully above the building's red tiled roofs and thought of that image and of the poignancy of Ivan's comment back then.

Stoker had brought his friend to the monastery at Ivan's request after the mission to the Transylvanian Mountains had almost killed him and left his men decimated. Stoker left Ivan in Brother Nicholas' care, and then in 1905, Ivan joined the monks, the Little Brothers of Christ, and had summoned Stoker back to explain why.

"The vampire's attack went hard with my men in the pass near the beast's castle until the sun rose," Ivan concluded, after going into much detail beforehand. "I survived and that undead thing did not get the journal, no, I hid it well before I left to get the final piece needed to confirm the creature's plans."

"But we must expose that loathsome creature's designs," Stoker pleaded, "before it's becomes too late."

"No, it isn't time yet, Sean," Ivan replied, then looked away, "so I must trust in God's will for now, so like Job," and Ivan tapped Sean's leg, "I can't go out into the world anymore, it is too dangerous. Even here I am watched," and Ivan glanced around nervously. After a few moments, when he thought it was safe, he continued, "Only from here at St. Constantine's can I oversee what must be done to finish the tasks of connecting the dots to the Black Hand's movement to thwart the vampire's mission. Do you understand?" Ivan's eyes had grown wide with a vivid fanaticism, but after few moments, he looked away and said no more. Knowing his friend well, it was quite evident to Stoker that Ivan wasn't yet ready to release the journal to the British ministry.

That had been in 1905, but it was now the summer of 1914, a season of beautiful, and lush days on the Continent and in England, but recent Balkan events threatened to shatter peace's illusions. The British Foreign Ministry had been working hard to prevent such a catastrophe and as Lord Grey had told Stoker in the Foreign Office, five days previous, "We are dangerously close to war, my boy, dangerously close. One major incident could explode the entire European powder keg that the Great Powers are sitting on," and he held up a telegram, "but sometimes the Almighty provides." Grey's tone sounded hopeful as he went on, "So, go out to St. Constantine's. Bring back Ivan's journal, and just maybe we'll get a half hour reprieve that might prevent this war." With those directives from Lord Grey, Captain Stoker had journeyed to the Balkans.

"Devil of a place to put a building," Stoker muttered as he stopped and leaned heavily on his walking staff while he looked at the monastery again. As an amateur engineer, Stoker admired the patience and endurance of these Eastern Orthodox clergymen in building up here. "Damn good view of the valley. Fine angles, all the approaches covered," he sputtered as he looked around, collected his breath, and decided to look at his pocket watch. 'Bout ten minutes to go, he thought, took a breath, sighed, and set off again.

When Brother Nicholas was sure of who it was on the trail, he left his perch and started down the corridor to the stairwell to begin his descent. In his right arm, he held a small bound bundle with a white label on the front. "He has come," Nicholas murmured, as he reached the stairs, then stepped down, smiled, and chanted, "He has come."

When Stoker reached the main entrance, he noticed the bell outside the doorkeeper's window. It was made of brass and had some Cyrillic lettering on it. He pulled the flax cord twice, and a deep, mellow tone sounded, then lingered as it crossed over the valley below. When no one answered immediately, Stoker rang the bell again and looked up towards a small window, by the door. Finally, an archaic face appeared at the dirty glass. The doorkeeper opened the wooden frame and began to speak quickly. Sean couldn't fully understand the man's local Slavic dialect, but the Irishman could see that the man was attempting to be friendly. "I don't understand you. I'm Irish. Irish," Stoker pleaded. "Do you speak English?"

"Yes, Irish, Irish," the doorkeeper replied. "I do speak some English."

"I'm Sean Stoker, Stoker," he continued. "Got Brother Nicholas' cable. Came as soon as I could," and then he paused. "Do you have the package?"

"Ah, Stoker. Good, good," but then the face disappeared.

"Blast, where's he off to?" Stoker ranted as he impatiently pulled the bell's cord roughly this time.

When the doorkeeper reappeared, his face showed some anger as he spoke, "I hear," and shook a finger at Stoker and pushed a brown bundle over saying, "Here."

Stoker grabbed the item, read the label, which was done in a fine English script. "To Sean Stoker, Esq. - Dublin," and recognized Ivan's hand writing immediately. Instinctively, Stoker reached into his pants pocket and pulled out a silver coin and slid it over the window's sill towards the doorkeeper.

The old man looked puzzled, and then a hurt expression crossed his face. Finally, he looked at Stoker tolerantly and said, "Put in there," pointing towards a slotted box near the window.

Stoker could read Slavic and above the box, in gold letters was, "For the poor." A sense of cheapness flushed over him, and by the time he looked back up towards the attendant to apologize, the man was gone. "Damn," Stoker sputtered so he turned, put the coin in, and began his journey back down the mountainside after he put the journal inside his coat pocket. Using his walking stick for leverage, he increased his pace despite the risk of falling. "Must get out of here before nightfall," he muttered as he glanced back up towards the monastery one last time, then raised his arm in a salute and hoped that Nicholas saw it.

Brother Nicholas was at the upper window again and saw Stoker's wave. "Hurry," Nicholas mumbled nervously for the sun was beginning to move past the mid-day mark in the sky, "hurry."

Two peasants in a nearby field paused in their work and watched with bored amusement at the descent of the stranger.

"He's going to turn an ankle," the thin peasant said to his companion as they noticed a cloud of dust trailing behind the departing visitor.

"Must be in a big hurry," the other replied, his tone nonchalant. "Wasn't that way when he went up there."

"Must be English," the first peasant, the older of the two said, his tone belligerent as he tossed his head that way.

"Or German," the younger countered and laughed heartily. "No difference there to us," he continued, "They're all just infidels."

"Same up there," the man with the large scythe responded as he defiantly pointed towards the monastery.

"True," the other countered as he spat in defiance. "We are a cursed land, but not for much longer."

"Allah be praised," the first peasant said reverently, "but we shall have our day, one day," then he went back to his tasks in the field.

The other man didn't reply but watched intently as the stranger got closer to the village. Finally when the laborer was sure the visitor had made it back, the peasant returned to his work. He was watching the rectory for his Master, for this peasant had long ago lost his faith in God. He served a new lord now, one bent on freeing the land from those in Christ's house up on the mountain, so this peasant had made a pact with the Devil's agent and so was lost to God. The peasant had been told to watch for a foreigner. Now that the stranger had come and left, the peasant would report all he had seen back to his master.

Upon Stoker's arrival at the local inn, he went directly to the front desk and rang the bell. When a man and woman appeared, Stoker said, "I'll need a cab, Herr Frank."

"Yes," the innkeeper replied, "you are leaving us so soon?"

"Indeed," Stoker answered, "events in Bosnia necessitate the end of my vacation."

"And where are you headed?" Herr Frank asked.

"The train station. I'll be down in a few minutes," then Stoker went up hurriedly to his room.

The innkeeper turned to his wife. "Damn, woman," he muttered quietly, "what can we do?"

"Tell the Archduke to go back to Vienna," she immediately shot back, "he's scaring away the tourists."

Herr Frank silenced her with a finger to his lips and nodded towards a guest sitting in the lobby and whispered, "Police." She snorted her disapproval, but fell silent. "Ready Herr Stoker's bill, woman," the innkeeper blustered loudly, "and I'll get the cab."

While Herr Frank left to find the local cabby, the only guest in the lobby peered intently over the top of his newspaper.

Stoker returned after a few moments, paid the bill in full, even for the days he wasn't staying and bounded out the front door where the cab was waiting. The trip to the rail station was rough, but when he arrived he told the ticket agent, "A first class ticket, north bound, to Budapest." Once on board, Stoker kept Brother Ivan's journal in his pocket, not allowing himself the curiosity of opening the package until he was safe on English soil.

Now as he sat in his train berth, Stoker thought back to 1904 and of his dead friend, of the times they had spent in the Balkans, of those days and nights, and of their efforts in the service of the British government to stem the Pan Slavic Movement directed by the Black Hand, with Russia's blessing. "The great game," Stoker had told Ivan just prior to the incident at the mountain pass with the vampire.

"Yes," Ivan responded, "and the Balkans is the Czar's chess board. India is only a ruse to distract your government from the real goal."

"Istanbul," Stoker replied excitedly. "I knew it, the Russians have wanted that port since the Crimean War."

"No," Ivan cautioned, "The Czar and his ministers are being played by the Black Hand. Those Serbian terrorists have sold themselves out."

"To whom," Stoker whispered.

"The Devil," Ivan said firmly as he saw the look of astonishment in Stoker's eyes. "Satan," Ivan continued confidently, "has greater plans for the world than a warm water port for the Czar, so let me tell you what I have learned," and it was then that Ivan revealed what he knew of the Black Hand, of the terrorists, and of Devil's agent, the vampire, and the plans being set in motion for the 20th century. "I confirmed much in my travels," he said. "I have names, dates, places. All is beginning to come together and that was why the Virgin Mary came to me and why, when the time is right after I return from the vampire's castle that I will show your Foreign Office these connections," and Ivan tapped the journal. "It is all here, recorded, but if the creature, that agent of Satan, kills me before I can get the final proof," Ivan said sadly, "I will get the book to you Sean." Ivan's tone was deliberate as he went on, "till then, it will be safely put away." Stoker nodded. "If you should ever get a cable from here with the passage," Ivan stated grimly, 'Now are the times which try men's souls,' you'll know I am dead and that you should come and bring my journal back to the British." Tonight, as Stoker sat in his train compartment, a firm knock on the door startled him from his remembrances.

"Ticket and passport," the conductor barked as he slid the door back harshly.

"Yes," Stoker responded as he reached in his coat pocket and found the papers.

The conductor checked the documents quickly and passed them back. "Thank you, Herr Stoker," then the conductor touched his cap and concluded by saying, "I hope your journey will be a pleasant one back home."

"Thank you, Herr Conductor," Stoker replied formally, and after the man left, locked the door. While Stoker settled in, he noticed that the setting sun was trailing off, creating fingers of red and orange hues amongst the clouds. The sight of this, along with the train's motions, reminded Stoker of the Irish Sea where he had learned to sail as a youth at his parent's seaside estate. It was there he had also been taught the mariner's advice that, tonight as he rode the train to Budapest, he began to recite. "Red sky at night, sailor's delight. Red sky in the morning, sailor takes warning." Instinctively, he yawned for it had been a long day, so he stirred himself, trying to keep awake. Think man, keep awake, he thought and then an old prayer, ancient in its history, deep in its expression of fear, entered his consciousness. "From ghosties and ghoulies and long legged beasties, and things that go bump in the night," he began to say, "Lord, deliver us!" With that, he settled in for what would be long ride to Budapest.

Meanwhile back in the mountains, the peasant had made his way towards the cave that was in the next valley over from the monastery. It had taken him most of the late afternoon and early evening to walk there, but he was on the last few meters that led up to the cavern. He held the lantern at arm's length so that its glow would illuminate the stony path and pressed on in the deepening darkness. He was almost at the hidden entrance when he called out, "Master?"

Only silence replied.

Once at the crevice that lead to the grotto, the servant ducked his head, entered, calling out, "Master!"

The word echoed in the vastness of the place.

"Master," the creature's servant exclaimed, "it is I?" but still no response came. "I have news," the Lost Soul called out. Just then, he heard a fluttering of massive wings so stopped, stood still, and waited expectantly, the lantern hanging by his side, its light dimly lighting the cavern.

THREE

LONDON

Captain Stoker had arrived safely in Dover in the early morning and while the train sped towards London, he finally had a chance to read Brother Ivan's journal. After arriving in London, Stoker went directly to the Ministry, and what he found there didn't please him. Stoker had been told to wait in the anteroom of Lord Grey's office and had been ordered to give the Journal to Lord Grey's personal secretary, and did, reluctantly. After an hour's wait, the Captain was ushered across the hall to the office of the Under-Secretary of Eastern Affairs, a civil servant by the name of Thomas Mitland. Stoker hadn't been expecting that and as he sat there, facing the prim bureaucrat, Stoker attempted to control his frustrations as the Under-Secretary spoke.

"Lord Grey has had much to deal with of late Captain Stoker." Mitland's tone was formal, curt, and high pitched. There were bags under his eyes, and he looked to Stoker like Mitland could use a good sleep. "This Balkans Crisis is getting out of hand," the diplomat said with a sigh, "and his Lordship is quite busy at the present."

"Yes, Mr. Secretary, I know that but that was why I was sent out there as a forlorn hope, one that his Lordship felt was necessary at the time."

Mitland eyed Stoker with some disdain, but said nothing.

"I was also directed, by his Lordship," Stoker continued on firmly, "to personally return Brother Ivan's journal."

"I am aware of Brother Ivan's file, Captain Stoker," he Under Secretary shot back, then paused, "but I must warn you, that I find Ivan's observations although interesting, well...," and Mitland hesitated as he leafed through the journal, then stopped, "well, highly suspect." The Secretary looked up into Stoker's eyes and posed a question twinged with some skepticism, "Do you find Ivan, reliable?"

"Yes," Stoker said without hesitation.

Mitland shook his head, closed the journal and said dismissively, "Quite."

Stoker fought back his anger.

"It does seem to me Captain Stoker," Mitland went on in a condescending fashion, "that Ivan's observations are quite implausible for our modern age."

"Sir," Stoker responded, "Ivan's revelations may seem so, but remember, we were dealing with a man whose religious conversion was quite strong, and they may have clouded his feelings, but not his facts. Ivan was an experienced agent and trained to go where the evidence led him."

"Yes, yes, Captain, I can see some proof of that," Mitland sounded irritated, then, with a flicker of his hand, exclaimed, "but surely you, as an educated man, a man of science, of reason, can't take stock in these legends," and he paused, "with this nonsense." The Under Secretary leaned forward and hunched over his desk. "Vampires!" The word was said with disbelief. "Do you really believe that old hokum?"

"What I believe about the old tales of that region is irrelevant," Stoker replied. "It is what Ivan documented that counts, and facts, as Tobias Smollet said, are stubborn things."

Stoker's voice had a steely quality to it that made Mitland pull back in his seat. "Ivan," Stoker continued, "had only become a monk after years of soldiering and fighting in the Balkan Wars. He knew, first hand, the horrors of war. Soldiers, Mr. Mitland, are not easily convinced, Sir, they are skeptics." Stoker could see that the Under-Secretary wasn't moving in his viewpoint, and the way his face was set didn't bode well for this line of argument so changed tactics. "No, I do not believe in vampires, but Ivan's account of a blond figure, of that figure's actions in the Balkans, is based on first hand interviews." Stoker could feel his passions rising as he pressed on. "Ivan had gotten inside the Black Hand and had become a reliable confidant of many of them," and Stoker lingered before making the next statement. "Then there is the encounter with the creature in Rumania, up in that damn pass. Ivan almost died that night and just barely made it back when I found him. It was his vision of the Virgin Mary that told him to seek out the monastery as a sanctuary, so I got him there and left him in the care of Brother Nicholas." The emotion in Stoker's voice was strong as he concluded. "You can call that blond creature what you will, Ivan called it a vampire. I, for one, can't discount that it wasn't, but I have known Ivan for a long time Sir, and he was not a man to rush to judgment. We cannot discount the evidence Ivan collected," and Stoker pointed to the journal, "and stored in there. We're lucky that beast didn't find it, so Brother Nicholas has done us a great service," Stoker said confidently, "and we have to use Ivan's evidence to alert His Majesty's Government as to the real danger in the Balkans!"

"Well," the Under-Secretary drawled as he reached for a glass of water near the edge of his desk, took it and sipped slowly, but said no more at this point.

Stoker felt that the man was stalling and decided to wait him out.

After a further lengthy pause, Mitland began to speak in a deliberate way, "Well, I will report our conversation to his Lordship," and the Under Secretary looked down at the other papers on his desk, waved his hand dismissively and said "thank you and I bid you good day."

"Sir," Stoker snapped, his voice rising as his temper flared, "I was told to see his Lordship, by his Lordship, so consequently I must speak to Lord Grey, in person."

The bureaucrat glanced up, his face flushed with anger. "That was before the Balkans got out of control," he declared as he thumbed his hand fiercely on the desk. "His Lordship is dealing with an immediate war with the Archduke's assassination and that is real, not this vampire theory of a dead monk." Finally Mitland flipped through the pages of Ivan's journal contemptuously, closing it harshly and exclaimed, "Now, Captain, again, I say, good day to you!"

Stoker was a seasoned enough soldier to see the futility of pursuing his present position so he rose from his chair and snapped out a smart, "Good day Sir," turned, and left. After he had gone down the hallway a bit, Stoker muttered, "Blast and damn!" and although a small oath, its echo was audible in the hallway. Several passersby turned to look, but didn't admonish him, for Stoker's countenance suggested that to do so would be foolish. He descended the staircase and once outside, stopped at the first landing and lit a thin cigarette. Mindless of the others around him, he began to blow a smoke ring, and for those entering and exiting the Ministry, it seemed a bit odd, this man standing there blowing smoke rings, but this was London and there were odd occurrences happening in these late summer days. After a few minutes while rain clouds gathered above, he felt better for pausing to grab a smoke, a trick he had learned from his first regimental commander in the Army.

"Keep your head when faced with a temporary loss, Lieutenant Stoker," the Colonel had said coolly one day after a field training exercise had gone badly for Stoker back in 1899. "Rashness can be useful if one can be calm about it. Why, even Wellington got rattled some, but he'd never panicked," the Colonel continued in a fatherly fashion, "not even at Waterloo. Sometimes, Lieutenant Stoker," the Colonel concluded, "a good smoke can give one time to reflect, so remember that," and then dismissed Stoker from the regimental office.

"Well," Stoker muttered out loud after his failed meeting at the Ministry today, as he threw down his half finished cigarette, "I think I have a plan in mind," and rubbed his chin in satisfaction and started down the Ministry's steps, headed towards a group of waiting cabs. "The Lodgings," he called out to the first driver in the line and tossed up a coin. "Quick as you can!"

"Watch your step, your lordship," the cabby barked out in a thick brogue as he caught the coin.

It had begun to rain slightly, and as the cab jolted off, Stoker was thrown hard into a plush wall. "Brash it out, Boyo," he sputtered as he caught his breath, "the game's a foot." Out of habit, he reached inside his coat for the gold cigarette case, one of the few personal keepsakes he had gotten upon his father's death. While Sean ran his fingers over the case, he felt the embossed crest of his family whose bloodlines ran back before the battle of the Boyne. There was royalty in his family, but Stoker didn't care for such since he was a man of action. "A true wild goose," his father's aunt had called Stoker just before he had joined the 33rd Foot, Wellington's old regiment, "and it will be the death of you someday, my boy, mark my words."

As Stoker looked out the cab's window, the vehicle seemed to flow in and out of the traffic, effortlessly, whisking by other transports, close, but never touching. "Like static electricity," he muttered. After awhile, he saw a familiar street sign just as the cab slowed gracefully, its destination quite close.

"Here we are, your lordship," the cabby sang out, his soft Irish lilt being quite distinctive again.

Stoker poked his head out the window. "Right," but cabby made no move as Stoker got out, nor did the driver make much of an effort when Stoker tossed up the tip. With a catlike precision, the cabbie nabbed the coin then touched his whip to his team of perfectly matched black mares and was off, without a word. It was then that Stoker caught a quick glimpse of the driver's blond hair that trailed slightly down to his shoulders. As quickly as Stoker had made this observation, he dismissed it, turned, and went up the steps of "The Lodgings" or the City Club, its official name. The club was housed in a sooty, gray granite structure of Georgian construction. Only the ornate, double doors of teak wood with their massive fittings gave an indication of the membership's status. The brass was polished, every day, and as he took hold of one of the handles, the door opened easily

As he crossed the threshold into the marbled foyer, he approached the Porter's Station, watched carefully by the attendant. "Captain Sean Stoker to see Lord Grey," Sean stated as he handed over his calling card, its fine paper's whiteness stood out on the dark wood of the window sill. Stoker had paid good money to have his cards printed there since only the finest paper available at Banner's shop would do, for it was there where all the finest members of London society had their printing done, especially important after his transfer from the 33rd Foot to the Irish Guards had gone through.

The doorman was an ex-Blues sergeant, Stoker could tell from the man's regimental pin in his lapel. As the attendant took the calling card and placed it on a polished serving tray, from the look on his face, Stoker could see the man was studying him. "Sign here please," he said as he opened up a guest book and held out a pen. After reading the notation he read out loud what it said, "Ah, Captain Stoker, Irish Guards to see his Lord Grey," and looked up, disdainfully. "His Lordship is not expected to arrive until seven, Captain," the doorman said. "You can wait in the guest bar. Down the hall on the left, if you please," and he pointed. "Do you have anything to check?" The question was not asked in a complimentary way.

"No," Stoker replied in a command tone, asserting his status as an officer to let the porter know his place.

"Very good then, Sir, " the doorman answered with a curtness only a senior NC0 could have acquired.

"Thank you," Stoker replied just as curtly. Since tipping wasn't proper at "The Lodgings," he didn't repeat the mistake he had made at the monastery. After going down a short corridor, he soon found an open archway that was marked "Guest Bar," and entered. The small room was made up of deep mahogany woodwork with crystal glass fittings on the ceiling and walls and had leather furniture strategically placed. The short bar had fine amber spirits arrayed on the bar's shelves and there was a hint of old cigar smoke in the air. As he approached the bar, he saw the bartender, dressed in a short red vest with white shirt and bow tie, polishing some cut crystal glasses.

"Can I help you, Sir?" the older man asked politely.

"Yes. I'd like a Glenlivet with a side of water."

The bartender then proceeded to find the appropriate single malt on the shelf and while Stoker looked around, he saw no one else in the room. When the barman returned with a tumbler half full of Glenlivet, a pitcher of water and a glass, there was no exchange of money; that wasn't done in the club, since guests were charged to the accounts of the members.

"I'm the guest of Lord Grey," Stoker said quietly.

"Yes," the barman responded and reached under the counter and took up a ledger, opened it, and began to write. When finished, he looked up and said, "Thank you, Sir."

After that exchange, Stoker found a winged chair by the door and positioned himself there so that he could see anyone coming down the hallway. As he leaned back and took a small sip of the single malt, he felt its warmth flow down into his chest, sighed resignedly, then took another sip and waited for his Lordship to arrive. He had finished his second whiskey by 5:30, but refused to take a third one as he lit another cigarette. It was around 6:45 when he heard voices in the hallway, one of which he recognized as Lord Grey. Leaving the newest smoke in the ashtray on the small table nearby, Stoker proceeded towards the main entrance where he saw Lord Grey, handing his coat to the porter. After getting near, Stoker began to address Grey in a firm voice. "Forgive this intrusion, your Lordship, but I must speak with you."

Grey's look, as he turned and acknowledged Stoker, conveyed neither anger nor approval, but was more a look of astonishment. Stoker had taken a major risk in coming there, but had to chance it since it would be ungentlemanly for the Minister to refuse at the club, at least that was what the Captain was hoping for. After a few awkward seconds Grey nodded towards a private door nearby. The doorman moved quickly towards it since he was use to interpreting gestures. After opening the door, he stood off to the side as Lord Grey, and then Stoker went in.

Upon entering Stoker noticed that the room was small with no windows. There was a round table in the middle with several chairs arranged about. A decanter of whiskey was set on a silver tray on the table with four tumblers of Waterford crystal arranged about, while a fireplace was off to one side, whose flames reflected in the glasses' facets. There were no paintings in the room, and although the darkly paneled walls had two small, shaded electric lights set upon them, it was not enough to brighten the room's Spartan decor. It was obvious to him that this was a room for serious discussions and not entertainment.

As they sat down, Grey reached towards the tray, poured two drinks and then passed one to Stoker. "Well," Lord Grey began as he motioned to Stoker, "begin."

"Your Lordship," Stoker began quietly, "Ivan was no fool," and Stoker took a sip from his glass. "He may have been a fanatic, but he was no madman."

"Yes, Captain Stoker, but you can't believe his journal, surely, now that we've both read it."

"Sir, if Ivan said there was a vile creature in Rumania plotting to exploit the region to bring about the millennium of Satan's reign, I believe him."

"Captain, the Balkans is full of lunatics," Lord Grey countered as he fingered his glass, took a sip, then shook his head and uttered, "Bismarck was right, it's not worth the bones of a single Pomeranian grenadier." Grey sighed heavily. "But the Iron Chancellor is not alive to help defuse this Bosnian affair now," Grey continued. "A madness has come over the leaders of today, and present events and mobilization plans threaten to put the lights out all over Europe," and Grey looked at Stoker and pointed a finger. "Those events, not some demonic plot, are real," Lord Grey, said firmly. "I can hardly believe that we are being manipulated by Lucifer, let alone his agent, a vampire."

Stoker made no counter to Grey's statement at this point.

"No, Captain," Grey continued, "this crisis between Serbia and the Austrian-Hungarians is the result of men who are stumbling into the abyss of war. Actions beget actions today, and timetables and war plans direct us now, not diplomats and statesmen. The crowned heads of Europe have lost control of the very machinery they were meant to break if events got out of hand." His tone was ministerial. "War is coming. It will be terrible," and Grey dropped his tone, "and I'm afraid." As he reached for his glass again, he stared into the tumble and after a few moments, his voice sounded calmer as he went on, "Do not suggest to me that when this war comes that is was the actions of Satan which caused it. This is the 20th century. Science has helped us discard the old ignorance. The only Devil we have here is ourselves. It is man who causes war, not Satan, Captain, and it is we who have chosen to go down that path. It is our madness that will put out the lamps in Europe and we can't go back." Lord Grey looked up and into the face of Captain Stoker and said, "It's too late now, too late."

Stoker had listened patiently but spoke calmly sensing that he had a chance now to counter Lord Grey's view. "I agree, your Lordship. War is looming, but we can still act to prevent it. Ivan's knowledge gives us one last chance. His evidence makes sense in light of the past 30 years of history in the Balkans. If we can delay these present events, even for a month, the greater evil of a second war among the Great Powers will not happen. That is the real danger in Satan's plot." Stoker's voice was taking on urgency as he continued. "We need time, even if it is only a few weeks. Rashness is what the vile creature wants. The Balkan crisis is the excuse to create a second world war thirty years from now. The warnings of Nostradamus are coming true, and Ivan's journal proves that Frenchman was right."

"I've read Nostradamus," Grey replied, as he looked into Stoker's eyes. "And I'm aware of the visions of the future since our agents in the Vatican have kept us informed, but I take no stock in such things. As a man of science, these projections of future events aren't scientific. What is predictable is the present course of events, and it will soon be too late to stop the military mobilizations being threatened since the Archduke's assassination at Sarajevo. Each nation sees those mobilizations as threats that can't be ignored. Even the Kaiser can't stop his General Staff from calling up the troop trains now, for it was swiftness of Prussian mobilization in 1870 which helped them in beating the French," and Grey stopped and pointed a finger again at Stoker. "The war of 1870 set a precedent that every major European country has learned since. Survival of the fastest," and the Minister shook his head. "The Austrians have been frustrated in the Balkans for too long, and want their pound of Serbian flesh. The Russians will react when their Slavic brothers are threatened, and so these armed camps will call upon their secret treaties with their allies. The Germans will aid their Austrian kindred, and the French will come in to protect Russia. We shall enter for self preservation since the Entente Cordiale binds us to the French, and so the late Queen's cousins will ignore their family ties and will war against each other for a house divided against itself cannot stand."

"Has King George asked his Imperial Majesty to intervene?" Stoker asked.

"Yes," Lord Grey replied, "and the Kaiser has got himself, once again, in a position of losing prestige if he doesn't honor his secret accords with the Austrians. He won't back down. Those military timetables," and before Grey realized he sputtered, "those bloody damn charts!"

Stoker was surprised by Grey's oath, but said nothing.

"Those Prussians live by them and his Imperial Majesty's General Staff will not let the Kaiser forget that," Grey continued as he gestured with one hand. "Now with the Austrian ultimatum to Serbia, the whole damn mobilization has begun and once it has started, its momentum will be irresistible. It's a mathematical progression we can't stop," and Lord Grey paused, a look of frustration on his face. "So, if you please, Captain, it has been a very long day, and I must eat something."

He had never seen Lord Grey plead before, and it was upsetting to Stoker so when he replied, his tone was tender, "I realize that, your Lordship, but," then Grey cut in.

"Yes, yes, Captain, I know but no more. Old and foolish men will make a war out of this, not the Devil. Our young men will fight and die, and I'm afraid, not much will be accomplished by the blood that will be shed, for this is the curse of our species, at times such as these."

"Only the Devil will win from this tragedy, your Lordship," Stoker replied in his attempt to convince Grey. "We have to act using Ivan's journal," Stoker pleaded. "We have to have the courage of our convictions."

"Perhaps, Captain, but we have to trust in goodness, not courage. We will find a way back, even after the war comes. We have made too much progress since 1870 to let it get destroyed by a general European war now. Our mission, then, is to end this coming war quickly. Then," Grey stated hopefully, "we can restore the continental balance with a new Concert of Europe so that, in the end, goodness will prevail."

"Goodness has nothing to do with war your Lordship. War is hell. Once the bloodletting starts, we can't control its impact. We must act now. Doesn't God help those who help themselves? Isn't that why Christ was sent to save us from our warring madness?"

"Perhaps," Grey said, "but it would seem that we have not learned very much in the past nineteen hundred years. A continental war awaits us, and it will involve all the major powers. It will be 1803 all over again, and no single man, or monarch, or government can stop it. We must trust that the days of fighting will be quick, and that victory will be swift."

"But your Lordship, Ivan's journal tells us that it will not be a quick war. The Virgin Mary told him just the opposite. This modern war, of automatic killing by machine guns, will be long and terrible. We will lose a whole generation of men to these infernal guns. Courage will count for nothing in the face of those guns. We must make the Kaiser and the Czar see that. Those who attack will die by the thousands. We must use Ivan's evidence to show them that."

"What makes you believe they will trust in Ivan's facts?" His lordship was sitting back in his chair, his shoulders drooping, his expression fading. "Their vision is distracted by prestige and ambitions," and he raised his hands slightly, palms up. "Now, if you please, Captain, I must have some serenity, even if it's just a good meal."

Stoker could sense that the debate was finally over, and so rose. He extended his hand. "Thank you for seeing me, your Lordship," and then Stoker waited.

"Quite," Grey snorted as he took the Captain's hand, then the Minister winked. "Had no choice, did I? Old school," and he bobbed his head at Stoker's tie, for each wore one in the same colors of their public school. Although Stoker hadn't counted on that, the school tie had played a part in Lord Grey's willingness to see the Captain. "Ties that bind," the Minister said, chuckling. Stoker smiled at this small jest. "Remember this, Sean," Lord Grey continued, "you cannot fight evil with evil or else you become a monster yourself in the process."

"Nietzsche?"

"Yes, but a paraphrase, I'm afraid. We can't use Ivan's journal presently, so like Job in the Bible, we shall endure for now, but I will make sure Ivan's journal isn't lost.

When the time's right," Grey said quietly, "we will let the cat out of the bag, so to say. Till then, we'll trust in God and keep our powder dry."

"Good night, your Lordship."

"Goodbye, Captain Stoker."

As Lord Grey came out of the private room, the porter asked, "Two for dinner, your Lordship?"

"No," Lord Grey said, his voice sounding weary, "just one."

"Very good, Sir, I'll ring for a waiter."

While Lord Grey stood there, presently a smartly dressed waiter appeared and said, "This way, your Lordship."

While the duo proceeded down the corridor, they came upon a formally dressed young gentleman with blond hair who stood by the main staircase. As he leaned against the newel post with flippancy in his posture that Lord Grey immediately noticed, the young man nodded. Grey nodded back, but didn't recognize the man though, and thought of speaking, yet decided against it for his Lordship wasn't in the mood for further idle conversation.

Once he had gone by, the stranger turned quickly and began to bound up the stairs, passing by two elderly members standing on the stair's first landing.

"Well now," the first member remarked to his companion, "did you hear that?"

"Quite," the second member snapped, "sounds like a cat's purr."

"Odd," the former chortled.

"Odd indeed, old boy, but these are odd days, odd,"

"Quite." In an instance, each dismissed the incident and proceeded down the staircase, headed for the dining room.

When Lord Grey entered the main dining room, he was shown to his usual table by a large window. "Seems warm in here tonight," he remarked to his waiter.

"Yes it does, Sir. Shall I open the glass?" the waiter asked.

"Won't be necessary," Lord Grey replied casually. As he took up the menu and absently mindedly glanced at the nightly carte du jour, the waiter stood patiently, off to the side.

While this was going on, Captain Stoker walked home in the misty London fog. Musing about what might have been if Ivan's journal had been brought to light, he finally concluded, there's nothing more to be done.

The vampire was also walking the shrouded streets, but it was looking for a blood feast to celebrate the coming war among the Great Powers. It was near the theater district when it spied a small flower girl near an alley. Like the beast it was, it approached her with grand anticipation, grinning sweetly.

As all these events played out, the Austrian ultimatum, set for the 25th of July, was fast approaching, and nothing earthly could stop it now.

FOUR

Before the guns of August boomed out in earnest and the slaughter of a generation began, millions in Europe had cheered the war's tragic opening. Unlike the war of 1870, the war that had begun in 1914 had a longer run than expected. In the conflict's fifth year, Adolph Hitler, a corporal in a Bavarian regiment, who had enlisted with a patriotic thrill that many others had felt in the early days, had so far endured and survived. He had experienced the ugly face of battle in the trenches of the Western front and had eventually become a battalion runner. His position as a runner, although dangerous, had been exciting, and helped filled the void in what, until then, had been a frustrated life. "Vital cog in a big wheel," he had told young Keital who had replaced Schuman, killed by a French sniper in 1916.

In 1917, Keital had been gassed in early spring when he had dropped into a shell hole to find cover. "Gas settles," they had been warned as new recruits, and by the time Keital had put his gas mask on, he had inhaled too much.

"Bad business that," the Major had remarked when Keital had collapsed in the dugout after he delivered the message, but by what strength of courage even the Major couldn't believe.

"Bad indeed," the dog-faced Sergeant snapped as they watched Keital writhing on the dirt floor. "Like drowning they say, Sir."

"Make sure to mention the lad in the dispatches, Sergeant," the Major replied with a nod.

"Yes, Herr Major," the Sergeant remarked as he wrote Keital's name down in the battalion's log.

"Damn bad luck," Hitler muttered to Kline, the new runner as they sat there witnessing this scene, waiting for their names to be called for the next mission.

"Will he make it?" the new man whispered.

"No," Hitler replied as they fell silent while waiting for the medical orderlies to come and take Keital away.

Kline was killed early in February 1918 by shrapnel well before the Americans had entered the war in strength and as a result, was replaced by Lang who was now missing. Consequently, Hitler, as an experienced messenger, had been sent out to see if he could find Lang, and when the shelling had let up some, Hitler discovered some remains that consisted of a boot and parts of smoking flesh and bone. Strangely, Lang's messenger case had survived, but the message had been blown to bits so Hitler grabbed the container and took it back.

"Looks as though a direct hit blew Lang to pieces, Sergeant," Hitler said as he reported in to the Duty Sergeant who took the container and noted that the message had been lost.

"Here," he said after writing out a new message, "give this to Major Feldman at the Divisional Artillery, two kilometers east of our position." Hitler took the new message and put it inside his container. "The Frogs are using gas tonight so be careful," the Sergeant stated as he tapped his own gas mask. "This is an important message, so make sure you get through."

"Yes, Sergeant." Hitler replied, then turned, and headed for the dugout's door.

"Watch out for raiding parties," the Sergeant said nonchalantly.

"Thanks," Hitler chirped as he waved, and then went past the blackout curtain and up the remaining steps into the dark trench. As his eyes began to adjust to the night sky, he felt inside his coat for his revolver and then touched his trench knife that hung on his belt. "All there," he mumbled, for messengers weren't heavily armed and mostly carried knives. Runners were suppose to depend on speed, silence, and cunning to get their messages through, not their fighting ability; yet Hitler carried a Luger pistol, just in case. He had been wounded twice and reported in regimental dispatches three times, but an official medal hadn't yet been awarded. In private, he anguished over this slight to his valor. He dearly wished to wear a medal's ribbon on his uniform, but as an Austrian in a German unit, rewards sometimes came slow. This was a reality he accepted, just as he accepted the necessity of getting this new message through.

As he made his way along in the main trench, the clouded sky was illuminated by the glare of flares that each side shot up. Even though the trench's level was deep, he half crouched as he moved along its re-enforced embankments. Like a rodent traversing through a maze, he navigated the trench's twists and turns, moving past sleeping soldiers, past quiet sentries posted to watch for trench raiders until he finally came to the communication trench. With less contortions in its design, they were more dangerous because of this and ran perpendicular to the main defensive lines and back to the secondary line, and usually, to a third or fourth series of defenses. Beyond these last trenches was the rear area where the billets were, along with the divisional artillery, and relative safety.

Tonight, the darkness Hitler had to navigate in was further enhanced by being below the earth's surface where distances were difficult to judge and where to raise one's head to get a reference fix was to invite disaster. Death was never very far away in the trenches, but the veteran runner moved smoothly along, scanning about, looking for movement ahead and slightly above. He always was vulnerable from the rear, but that fear was something all runners had to deal with.

"Trust your senses," they had been told when first schooled in the ways of runners. "If your neck hairs stand up, that's normal, but it's when you feel safe, watch out. The enemy will watch till you pass, then, drop from behind," the instructor had said, "so if you're jumped, you must not panic - use your knife. Stab at anything and try to keep moving." In acquiring the mastery of his job through experience, Hitler had learned another valuable lesson, so he always carried a pistol lightly tucked in his tunic. The flash of the gun, the noise it created in the trench's confined spaces, especially at night, could allow a runner an edge in a fight, and so, perhaps, a chance to get away.

"Chance is fickle in war," he had told Lang once, "it shows no respect for rank, but any opportunity to survive in this war is worth taking."

Just then, as Hitler moved along tonight, a flare burst overhead. He stopped. When the flare drifted away and its light began to fade, he started to move again, but the beast, like a good hunter waited. While the messenger passed by, the vampire began to purr softly in anticipation.

In the instance between when one flare's light died and another was shot up and burst, in that moment, the vampire struck. It leaped upon the Corporal's back from behind and grappled with the runner.

Despite the impact, Hitler pulled his pistol out and fired. The Luger's muzzle flashed brightly as several quick rounds burst out. If Hitler had fought a man, this would have worked, but the beast knew this trick and so had designed the attack to deal with it.

By the time the Corporal had finished firing two rounds, the beast had swung around and struck from the other side. This time, it pinned its prey face down into the trench's wooden flooring and, immediately, the beast expertly exposed the man's neck. Instead of making the stroke that would quench its hunger, tonight, the vampire had another objective in mind for it had been watching this particular runner for a long time during the war and knew that his soldier was a survivor. The beast now knew too that if the runner could be put on the right path, he would become a convert to Satan's plans, and would become the Chosen One.

Meanwhile, Hitler lay helpless in the mud, thinking only of the here, of the now and would his enemy choose life or death?

The beast bent lower and whispered into the Corporal's ear. "Now, little brother, listen. We have little time so you must choose. Will it be glory and Satan, or God?"

The Corporal's mind went wild. Had he heard correctly?

The beast didn't repeat the question as it tightened its grip a little.

"Glory." The reply was muted and raspy.

The beast to growled its disapproval and tightened its grip.

"Glory and Satan," Hitler finally gasped in a near panic whereupon the beast lessened its grip some as the light from the most recent flare faded.

"Good, good," the vampire cooed, then it struck, sinking its fangs into the man's neck just enough to cause Hitler to swoon. While the beast and victim's essences mingled, the bond was made. Finally, the creature drew back. "There," it said and licked its fangs like a gourmet appreciating its meal, "we are one in body and mind."

Every sense in the soldier's body was in a stat of frenzy, for the beast still rode the man's back and wouldn't let its victim up. "Listen," it said speaking quickly, "you will survive this war and you will return home. You will become a spy for the government and join the National Socialist Party too and from that membership, the world will be open to you," and the vampire paused briefly. "Watch the Turks. See how they will destroy our ancient enemies, the Armenians, then use that lesson to go after the European Jews, for in their persecution, you will gain power since the Jew is already hated, so use that." Hitler was breathing hard, but listening intently. "Spread the word of purity, of Aryanism - build upon it," the vampire whispered. "Talk of a new order, a new Reich, of a 1,000 years reign. Satan will provide," and the vampire's voice was silky, "and I will be there for you, always near at hand." The beast rose slightly, anticipating a new flare about to be sent up. "You will have only three decades to do these things." It stood up and pointed a finger at the prostrate man. "Remember, three decades," and with that, it rose off its feet, just as a new flare began to ascend. "Remember, I am with you," and as the flare burst brightly, the vampire was gone.

How long Hitler lay there trying to recover, not knowing if what had happened, of what had been foretold, was real, but when his hand finally reached to his neck, he felt wetness there. "Blood," he mumbled and looked around, but saw no living person in the trench. Clumsily he drew himself up, stumbled forward and eventually reached the artillery reserve battery headquarters that was situated in a wrecked barn. He was covered in mud, hair tossed and face whitened as he tried to stand at attention. "Sir," Hitler said as he thrust out the container towards the Duty Sergeant. "Message from battalion."

The Sergeant took the pouch, opened it and handed the message to Major Feldman who began to read it by the dim light of a covered lantern.

"Good work, Corporal," Major Feldman finally said as he looked up from the paper and cocked his head. "You seem to have been wounded?"

The runner nodded.

"There's blood on his collar too, Sir, probably shrapnel," the sergeant added.

"Yes, well," Major Feldman replied, "let's get this man to the Aid Station, Sergeant. Now, what's your name soldier?

"Corporal Adolph Hitler, Herr Major."

"Note that in the book, Sergeant, for this is a vital message," and Feldman slapped the paper. "I'll see he's proposed for the Iron Cross," the officer proclaimed with a smile. "We need good yeoman like Hitler here! Not many of the old hands left, hey, Corporal."

Hitler could only nod as he gazed at Major Feldman.

"Orderly," the Duty Sergeant called out.

Within a few moments an Orderly appeared. "Yes, Sergeant?"

"Take this man to the aid station," the Sergeant commanded.

"This way comrade," the medical attendant said as he put his arm around Hitler.

"Thanks," he replied and sagged into the Orderly's arms. Once outside, they had gone only a few meters when the divisional artillery began to fire, but the sounds of out going shells held no fear for the runner, for there was a comfort in knowing those whines. Veterans learned early the difference from outgoing and incoming rounds, and Hitler thought of Lang again. "The ones you don't hear," Hitler had told Lang with a laugh, "well, don't worry about them." As Hitler was helped along now, he thought, I wonder if Lang heard the shell that got him but for some reason, the memory of the Lang left Hitler's thoughts, and a new idea came to him. "A medal," he muttered over the sound of the battery's guns, "the Major said I'd get a medal."

"What's that you said," the attendant asked, "what?"

"A medal." Hitler replied smiling like a child. "The Major said I'd get a medal for this."

"Yes, a medal," the Orderly answered, then added coyly, "It's has been a good night now, so come," but before they had gone much farther, Hitler fainted. Instantly, the attendant stopped, shifted Hitler's weight easily, swept him up, and carried him the last 40 yards into the Aid Station.

"Over there," the doctor on duty said as the attendant came inside. Recent casualties hadn't been heavy, but they had been constant due to the French artillery fire so the tired doctor was not happy to see a new patient brought in. Consequently, he spoke bluntly as the Orderly placed the wounded man on a cot, "We'll get to him."

The Orderly turned. When he spoke, it was with an ominous, deep tone, "Now, Herr Doctor."

Startled at being spoken to in such a tone, the doctor looked up from the patient he was working on and thought of speaking harshly back, but there was something there in the eyes of that Orderly which frightened the man of science. When the doctor's reply came, it was weak, and characteristically unlike himself. "Yes, I will."

The attendant smiled, then left without a glance back.

After that, the doctor went to the new wounded man's cot and examined him. "Odd," the physician uttered as his fingers reached for the neck wound, "only these two small neck punctures," and then he called out, "Nellenback?"

From the other side of the tent, a medical assistant, who had witnessed the whole previous scene, came over. "Sir?"

"Bring a medical tray," the doctor commanded. After Nellenback returned, the doctor moved Hitler's head slightly to the side and said, "Look at these two wounds."

"Yes, Herr Major, very neat and precise. Shrapnel?"

"Probably, but they aren't very deep, so dress them," and then doctor got up. "Then, let the Corporal sleep."

"Very good, Herr Doctor."

"Is it warm in here?" the doctor asked as he wiped his brow.

"Yes, now that you mention it," Nellenback responded as he began to work on the wounded man's neck, "it does."

"Well then, open the tent's flap when you're done."

"Yes, Herr Doctor, I will."

The German battery's artillery fire was increasing now, the reverberations shaking the ground. The effect was causing some of the wounded in the hospital ward to call out in fear and fright.

"Things could get heavy again," the doctor began as he jerked his thumb towards the sounds of the guns. He looked at Nellenback. "See what supplies we have left after you done there." After the doctor returned to his other duties, this latest wounded man was forgotten about. The uneasiness the doctor felt from this incident, however, couldn't be so quickly dismissed, and in the following nights, he would reflect on that blond Orderly and his piercing eyes. The image of that soldier would haunt the doctor's sleep, causing him much distress and discomfort, for weeks to come.

FIVE

By the summer of 1918, Sean Stoker had seen many a friend "go West," yet he had survived, and his valor at the front hadn't gone unnoticed for he was now a major, 2nd Battalion, Irish Guards. He had been wounded several times, gassed once and his medals, if he chose to wear them, would have festooned his uniform. Stoker wasn't in London on leave, he was at the front again, deep inside the battalion dugout trying vainly to rest before leading the raid tonight, but a tune's humming stirred his fitful slumber. He recognized the song, it was an old march, *Around the Mall*, a prewar favorite, and as he turned in his cot, he saw his friend, Lieutenant James Delaney, Jimbo as Stoker called him, seated at a makeshift table of Army ration boxes. Delaney was checking over Stoker's gear for the upcoming raid.

Ordinarily, a lieutenant or a captain would take the party out but tonight, Stoker chose to. In the Guards, field officers were expected to lead, they weren't rear area types who sat in French chateaux, sipped champagne, and wore the red tabs. There was a wide gully between line officers and the red tab staff officers, and often, front line soldiers felt that the real enemy was the staffers, and tension ran high between the two groups. "Damn Red Tabs," the men would grumble if one of the staffers appeared at the front, and it was for that reason Stoker had turned down a staff job. "Duty means more than a tab," he had told Delaney once. "We lead by example and the men respect us for that," which was why Stoker was going to lead the trench raid tonight.

"Evening, Major," Delaney said as he noticed Stoker swinging his legs over the side of the cot. "It's a good night for it."

"And the moon?" Stoker asked gently.

"Hidden by a lovely cloud layer. Very thick." Delaney was Irish too and had come out with the battalion in 1915.

"Has Sergeant Smithe chosen the raiding party?" Stoker mumbled as he rose.

"Yes. Dougherty, Andrews, Matthews and Glendon."

"Good," Stoker muttered as he stretched, then started to come over. "Headquarters thinks the Germans are up to something, despite the peace negotiations."

"We still have to teach those lads over there a lesson, Sir," Delaney answered grimly. "They're an arrogant lot, those Prussians, even the Kinder they're sending out these days."

"Boys, Delaney, there still just boys," Stoker answered wearily as he reached for a cup of tea from a pot on a small field stove.

"True, but they'll kill you dead just as well," and he let his statement dangle there and when it drew no reply, he finished with the gear's assemblage. "All set," he continued once it was complete and added, "You'll present a fine figure to the Huns tonight, Major, a fine and proper specter."

Stoker gave a forced laugh, but neither acknowledged it. Each had had a disquieting feeling about tonight's raid ever since HQ sent the order down to get some new prisoners, especially regarding a blond German who had been raiding the British lines of late.

"Where's my gas mask?" Stoker asked as he looked about.

"Over on the wall," and Delaney rose and went to the wall peg.

"Any recent reports on that blond German?" Stoker inquired as he put his cup down and took his black balaclava from the table.

"Yes," Delaney answered while the Major strapped on his web belt and patted his pistol's holster. "Appears," Delaney went on as he returned, "that Fritz has been active in our sector, again."

"Queer fellow," the Major muttered as he adjusted his balaclava, "especially how he seems to disappear so quickly, reminds me of someone Ivan and I ran into in the Balkans, before the war," but before Delaney could reply Stoker added, "Well, make sure to brew up some fresh tea."

"I will," Delaney replied as he tipped his fingers to his temple. This gesture was a part of their ritual observance before an event because soldiers are a superstitious lot.

"Cheerio," Stoker cried just before he went past the blackout curtain and up the dugout steps. At the top, he turned left, passed the first sentry, then down the trench, by a second guard, then further on, and past a third sentry. At that point, he turned right around a corner and found the raiding party. They were huddled together, all wearing dark woolen face masks, all lightly armed with trench knives, pistols and some grenades. An observer was on a raised step and peered into the overcast night with a camouflaged twin lens periscope.

In a hushed tone, Sergeant Smithe, a veteran, greeted Stoker. "All ready Major."

"Good." he answered, and moved up close to the observer. "How's it look?"

"The occasional flare, but a good night. Regiment reports some German activity," and added, nervously, "could be that blond Fritz, again."

"Thanks," Stoker replied, and turned to Smithe. "Ready, Sergeant?" He nodded, after which Stoker addressed his men. "Twenty second intervals. First two, ready, on my mark, 5, 4, 3, 2, 1, go," and up they went on the scaling ladders and over the trench's top and down on their bellies, two wiggling forms hugging the landscape. Stoker continued his silent counting and when he spoke again it was the same, "Next, 5, 4, 3. 2, 1, go," and out went two more. Again, Stoker counted silently and when it was time, he looked at the only raider left. "Ready?" The soldier flashed a smile and out they went. Once reassembled at the Listening Post, the raiders waited while Stoker moved up to one of the two sentries and whispered in his ear, "Anything?"

"No," he muttered and motioned with his head to his left, "See the steeple?"

The Major tapped the sentry's shoulder then drew back and returned to his men. He could see their misty vapors rising in the damp night's air as he spoke. "The church is off to the left. Be there by 0200. Password is 'Grave.' Counter sign, 'Matters.'" He then pointed to the nearest raider. After they crawled out of the hole, they snaked along until they came to a section of their own wire. There they found the small gap under the entanglement that the British used to gain access beyond their barbwire. Carefully, they crawled through and entered No-Man's Land.

By keeping low, each pair of raiders pushed on and were soon heavily soiled with dirt, water, and remains of both humans and animals since the previous fighting in that sector had left a cornucopia of Death's fruits all around. After a long while, the Major and his companion fell into a large shell hole. While they went through the goo at crater's bottom, trying to cross over to the other side, they had to fight the urge to vomit. Stoker's thoughts went back to a conversation he had with Delaney once. "It's surprising how much a man can get used to up here at the front, Jimbo."

"That's true enough," he had remarked, "and that's what the most frightening of all, Major."

Then, like a veteran soldier, Stoker dismissed his brief recollection tonight, just as quickly as the torso of the dead soldier he shoved away. Focus, his mind cried as the two raiders pushed their way to near the top of the large shell hole. Once at the edge, he signaled to stop and looked over and pointed at himself. His companion, Private Dougherty, nodded and immediately Stoker inched up, peered above the rim for several seconds. After he came back down, he whispered, "Ready?"

"Right," Dougherty muttered.

"Move to the left," Stoker answered, "and look for the steeple," and Dougherty nodded and then they went over and out. The ground was fairly even now so the two men began to run in a half crouch towards the ruined church that was about 40 yards away. The enemy, if they were inside would open up soon, each knew, but as the raiders dashed forward, no gunfire greeted them. After they got inside, the Major signaled Dougherty to stay there and watch, then the Major made a quick tour of the immediate ruins. The church had changed hands many times in the past year but now it was securely in No-Man's Land. Since the Armistice Talks, not much had been happening in this area of the front, but recently several nasty raids led by a blond German had occurred which indicated to the Headquarters' staff that the enemy was changing the status quo, so consequently, the rear echelon wanted to find out why, which meant new prisoners had to be obtained.

While the Major went quickly over the ruins, at least what one man could cover in a sweep of a minute or so, Dougherty kept his vigil. When Stoker got back, the other members of the raiding party hadn't arrived yet so he cupped his hand over his watch and with a small light from his kit to mask the light's beam took a quick look. "O230," he mumbled, shut the light, and then tapped Dougherty's shoulder. "They're late."

He held up his hand and muttered, "Something," and he pointed out to his left while he raised his pistol.

"Right," Stoker answered as he reached for a grenade in his pouch bag.

Within seconds, a distinct form took shape as it rose up from a shell hole and advanced. Within a few seconds, right behind, two more emerged and it looked as if they were dragging something.

"Grave," the foremost figure cried out, as he got closer.

"Matters," Stoker called back as the first soldier came staggering in to the ruined church. Within seconds, the others did as well, dropping what they carried. Stoker looked at the lead man, it was Sergeant Smithe and there was something in his eyes Stoker had only seen once before, a fear in the Sergeant's eyes, but Smithe was controlling it, just barely for now.

"Jerries jumped us," he said as he bent over, gasping for air. "We got a prisoner but lost a man, but I think we got'em all though."

"'Cept that blond bloke," a new voice cut in sharply. "Saw Matthews put a knife in that Hun bastard, right in his heart, but that Kraut picked Matthews up, snapped his back, and then boomin' just disappeared."

"Quiet there, Andrews," Smithe snapped.

"I saw it to Sarge," Private Glendon said. "That Fritz was fast."

"And those bloody eyes," Andrews shrieked. "Christ Jesus!"

"Steady lads," the Major replied for he felt the panic of his men building after their encounter. "Get a hold!" He turned to Dougherty. "See anything?"

"No."

"All right," Stoker said, trying to act calmly. He turned back to his other men. "Now, Andrews you watch over there," and pointed to the left. Just then a deep and painful moan erupted from the figure on the ground. Immediately, Private Glendon knelt down and cupped his hand over the wounded enemy soldier's mouth.

"Prisoner." It was Sergeant Smithe. "The Hun's bad sir, but we brought him with us anyways."

The Major went over and quickly assessed the prisoner and muttered, "Damn," for Stoker knew he'd have to make a decision fast. The raid's a dud, admit it and get back, he reasoned, then squared his chin and knew he had to make a choice. "Put a cloth around the prisoner's mouth," Stoker ordered, "but not too tight. We'll take him with us. Sergeant, you'll go first. I'll go next with Andrews and we'll carry the prisoner. Glendon will follow us for our relief and Dougherty's rearguard. Now get ready to move."

"Sir," Smithe replied thankfully, for an order spoken with confidence when men are near panic can help stop its spread. That's why Stoker's a good officer, Smithe thought as he looked about confidently now.

"Clear?" Stoker muttered to Dougherty, who nodded back. Quickly, Stoker pointed to Smithe and said, "Go," and without hesitation, he moved back into the void of No Man's Land, taking the lead for the returning raiders. A few seconds after he left, the Major looked back to see if Andrews and Glendon were ready and in those split seconds, the beast struck. It had come in low along the foundation of the church and when it was near Dougherty, it rose, grabbed the startled soldier by the neck and, before the man could fire off a round, ripped off his head. Like a whirlwind, it came through the wall's gap, shoved the Major forcefully aside and into the wall and was by Andrews instantly. With one swipe of the vampire's hand, it sliced open the soldier's throat and dropped him gasping on the top of the wounded German. Meanwhile, Glendon had pulled out his pistol and was firing point blank into the thing's face. The weapon's massive slugs would have knocked down a man, but on the vampire came through the gun's blast, grabbed Glendon by the neck and sunk its fangs into the poor man's jugular. After it fed, the beast discarded the body like a tin of finished sardines on top of Andrews and the German.

During the melee, Stoker lay stunned at the base of the wall until the beast finally turned, came over and just sat there, on its haunches, at Stoker's feet. As their eyes met, Sean saw the reddened stare of his enemy and felt drawn to its eyes. As Stoker pulled off his face mask with his undamaged arm, he recognized who it was and gasped, "You!"

The beast smiled, its fangs bright with blood. "Time to choose, little brother, God or Satan," but the Major could make no reply just then. In his heart, as a combat soldier, he was always prepared to die, that was a soldier's duty, but to face this thing, for that, Stoker wasn't prepared. "Now," the vampire hissed impatiently. At that prompting, Stoker closed his eyes and muttered, "God."

The vampire's lunge came quickly, and as it fed, it felt satisfied. When it finished, it stood up and surveyed what it had done while a feeling of immense gratification washed over it. "Well, little brother," the beast crowed as it looked down at Stoker's body, "Ivan and you are with your God." With mocking laughter, it rose above the carnage, spread it wings, and flew straight up into the gathering rain clouds, swirling and twisting like a ballroom dancer.

Eventually, the wounded German, Private Ludwig Miller, forced his way clear of the slaughtered corpses and saw Stoker's body up against the wall. Miller had seen the killing of the Major and, in horror, as the German began to crawl away, he heard a small moan. Could the Tommy still be alive? "Comrade?" Miller whispered as he dragged himself towards Stoker. "Comrade?" then the German tugged at Major Stoker, "Comrade, vas is dat?"

"Vampry," the Irishman moaned as he opened his eyes, ever so slightly.

"Vampry," Miller replied, his voice showing his disbelief, "Vampry?"

"Ya, Vampry," Stoker exhaled, grabbed his enemy's tunic with a final burst of strength, and shrieked, "Remember," and died.

While Miller looked into wild eyes of the dead corpse, the German urgently tore Stoker's hand away. After that though, an unexplained urgency overcame Miller so he groped the corpse to find any small item, anything, to prove what he had witnessed and survived had been real. Finally, he found a small St. Christopher's medal pinned to the Stoker's shirt and taking it, the German clenched it in his fist and began to crawl away. He didn't look back for he was afraid to look back, and once out beyond the ruins of that church, he only knew he had to get away before that thing, that fair-haired creature, came back. While a gentle misty rain began to fall all round, nothing else, not even the pain of his wounds, nor the increasing wetness of his uniform was on Miller's mind, his only urge was to escape.

After the incident at the church, Miller somehow crawled back to his own lines and was rescued. Luckily, he was sent to a base hospital, miles behind the lines, where a pretty female nurse, a Catholic nun, was the one who finally got him to open his hand. "What do you have there?" she asked quietly one day as she held his hand that he had clenched for days. For some reason, today, he responded to her kindness and opened his fist. "Ah, St. Christopher," she said, her voice angelic, "I can see why you keep him close." She then took the medal. "Now, let's pin it to your shirt and let the good Saint help with your nightmares."

Miller smiled weakly as she put the medal on and from that day onwards, he kept the medal pinned to his undershirt. In the following weeks of his recovery, whenever the vision of the beast haunted his dreams, he looked at the medal and tried to fight the nightmare off. He never told anyone about that church, about the enemy officer, or about the beast the British soldier had called a vampire, for who would have believed it?

SIX

After the Armistice, Hitler had returned home not to the place of his birth, but to his adoptive Fatherland wearing his medal, but things weren't good in the former lands of the deposed Kaiser. The old order of Imperial Germany was gone replaced by the democratic Weimar Republic. The immediate postwar upheavals from the Spartacus Uprisings in Germany to the new war between an independent Poland and Communist Russia had a traumatizing impact on the Germans' psyche. Average people just tried to survive, and like many, he too learned to cope, but he had one advantage most Germans didn't, he remembered what had been foretold that night in the trench and so waited. He joined the small Nazi Party first as a spy but soon became an ardent convert. He had risen in the Party's ranks and remarkably became its dominant force, the Fuhrer which seemed appropriate that he had lived up to his real name in German, Adolph, which meant Wolf.

In 1923, too, former Corporal Ludwig Miller was finally making a life as a waiter in Munich, and it was from the restaurant's window, on November 9th, that he witnessed the Putsch that General Luderndorff and Hitler attempted to overthrow the Bavaria state government. If successful, these two hope to launch a strike against the fledgling Weimar Republic, and if successful, to takeover all of Germany. Miller had seen the crowd of Nazis and their supporters gathering in the streets earlier in the day and after that, he witnessed the mob's advance on the government buildings. Luderndorff, the old World War I hero, was out front, while Hitler, who had risen to the leadership of the Nazis, slunk just behind. When the police arrived, shots were fired, and the pathetic coup was quickly put down with 16 Nazis, mostly men from the Brown Shirts, killed in the gunfire.

"That was fast," Miller muttered as the police dispersed the crowd, arresting Luderndorff in the process, "but I see Herr Hitler has escaped though," and pointed out the famous Nazi who was being spirited off towards a waiting black Mercedes, its rear windows shaded.

"Yes," Willie Schmidt, another waiter and war veteran replied as he stood by Miller, "and Herr Block's car is there to protect Hitler, just like a guardian angel would."

"I've not met Herr Block," Miller said.

"He's a regular of mine," Schmidt answered as the car carrying Hitler sped away. "Unusual to see Block in the day time though. Only comes in at night and sometimes we talk, politics usually, but one has to be careful to ones customers," Willie continued as he glanced around, "a false face is good these days."

"Why false?" Miller responded in some puzzlement.

"Why you never know," Schmidt answered, a sly look on his face as he nodded towards the last of the commotion in the street, "who will be running Germany in the future. In our crappy business, we serve all. Tips can be lost in a casual remark so keep your politics to yourself, and let each customer have an image of what they want to see, hen?" then as Miller nodded, Schmidt concluded, "A good waiter is friends to all," and he swept his hands about. "The customer is always right! Remember that, even if you serve a Nazi like Herr Block, or an aristocratic Prussian Junker, or a wealthy industrialist, or even the occasional fat Jew! Now," Schmidt concluded, "let's get back to work."

Consequently over the next few months, Miller kept his politics to himself and played the role of friendly waiter to all. With some extra money he had made in tips, he had also begun to take flying lessons, a desire he had had ever since he had been in the trenches in World War I. As he came back from a flight lesson from a small Munich airport one day after Hitler's failed coup, Miller thought of his dead friend Hans Beyermeister. It had been in the summer of 1918, as rumors of an armistice to end the war abounded when, one afternoon, Miller pointed to a German observation plane. "That's what I want to do and that will be my ticket out of this muck."

"Ya, Ya, Miller," Hans replied with a laugh, "and away from all this luxury and shit I suppose." Just then an incoming enemy shell started to drop towards their position. With the knowledge of combat veterans, they ducked just before the shell hit nearby, and after it missed them, Hans exclaimed with some dry humor, "See, even the enemy doesn't want you to fly away now."

"I will though," Miller muttered as he smiled through the dust on his face, "and I've already put in my application for the air service."

"Shut up you two," a sergeant growled as he came by. "Check your gear. Be prepared for gas and listen for the whistles for our assault."

After he moved down the trench, checking his men as they waited to begin the new counterattack, Hans looked carefully at his friend, "This new attack is stupid!"

"Ya," he answered, "and so is this war now!"

"Good luck," Hans said, then Miller gave the thumbs up.

"Get ready," the sergeant called out as he started to move towards the trench's ladder, "and listen for the signal." When the whistles broke out along the German lines, up went a gray wave, rolling forward into No Man's Land. It was the last time Miller saw his friend alive for he was cut to ribbons by machine gun fire on the enemy's wire, his arms hanging there as his torso fell back. After the failed assault, Miller made it back to his own lines safely, despite his wound.

"Lucky it's only a grazing," the Medical Attendant said as he examined the head wound, "lot's of blood, but nothing serious." After Miller was bandaged up, he was sent to the rear and tagged there as "Walking Wounded" and stayed until a doctor made his round of the wounded.

"We need men at the front," he said after examining Miller, "there's just not enough of us left." Finally, the doctor shrugged his shoulders, handed a release form over ordering Miller back to the front, and walked away.

When Miller reported in at his old battalion's headquarters, he asked the Duty Officer if the letter authorizing a transfer to the air service had come. "No," was the curt reply. "Report to your old company." He glanced at Miller with a resigned look, "We need all we can get, now." Miller knew that Germany was losing badly in this 5th year of the war and so just nodded and reported back.

Within a few days after that, a trench raid was ordered against the British in that sector of the German defenses. It was that raid which would influence his life forever. As a tall, blond major was making the selection of men fit enough for the raid, when he got to Miller, the major glared hard into Miller's eyes and snapped, "and you too! Be ready in five minutes."

"Yes, Herr Major," Miller replied nervously, for he didn't like the look in the Major's eyes. Just my luck, Miller thought, but he survived the raid that fateful night and the frightening incident at the church. Now, after the war, he was finally pursuing his dream of being a pilot and that felt satisfying.

Several days later, as Miller came to the restaurant in Munich to work the day shift, Schmidt was in the kitchen talking boldly to a group of employees. "A nice brown uniform, food and a future, now that's the life boys. You should think about joining up."

"What are you talking about," Miller interjected.

"I'm leaving this crap hole and joining the Brown Shirts."

"The paramilitary arm of the Nazi Party, but why," Miller asked in disbelief, "we have work here."

"But it won't last," Schmidt countered, his voice sounding confident, "and that's why the Brown Shirts are not a bad deal, Miller, not half bad at all, especially in the unsettled times that will come according to Herr Block. He has convinced me that even after this failed coup, Herr Hitler is the future. It is the Nazis who offer the young, like us, a chance to replace the Old Guard that the war destroyed, not this stinking Weimar Republic imposed on us by foreigners."

"But the Weimar Republic is succeeding," Miller countered, "and besides, Hitler has just been jailed."

"He won't' be there long," Schmidt countered, "not according to Herr Block."

"Who?" asked a new waiter who had just been hired.

"He's a regular here," Schmidt replied. "Quite a charming fellow once you get to know him, and he finally convinced me that The National Socialists are the future."

"Isn't he that blond fellow who sometimes comes in here at night?" the young dishwasher interjected.

"Yes," Schmidt answered "and now I plan to be a part of the Nazi Party and so should you all too."

"No, Schmidt," Miller replied, "the National Socialists aren't for me."

"Too bad, but according to Herr Block, the Nazi are the future, but you're still a fine fellow anyways, Miller," Schmidt replied as he put out his hand. "Well," he continued, "good luck, Ludwig."

"And good luck to you too," he answered as they finished shaking hands.

"We make our own luck, remember that," and then Schmidt waved to the remaining staff and, with a flourish, opened the door and strode out.

"I wonder if he's right," the dishwasher remarked after Schmidt left.

"Ya," another waiter interjected, "but the Jews won't let us live in peace."

"Nor the Communists," another interjected, "look at what they're doing in Russia under Lenin and Stalin."

"That's the Poles problem for now," another waiter said.

"We'll take Danzig back," the senior waiter snapped angrily. He too was an Army veteran and bitter about the war's results, especially since the transfer of that German port city to the newly created Poland. "One day, we take all of Poland too."

"Can Hitler do all of this?" the former asked.

"Hitler's a true patriot and so is Herr Block," the senior waiter said, "so we'll see, but let's get to work; the day crowd will be coming in soon."

As the wait staff began to attend to their duties, Miller kept his remaining thoughts to himself and tried not to think of political things, just work occupied his mind and the tips he hoped to collect to use for his continuing flying lessons. For some reason though, the mentioning of Herr Block caused old war memories to stir in Miller's mind and as he went about his tasks, he finally put his hand inside his shirt, felt for the St. Christopher medal and tried to calm himself for the day's work ahead.

It was the Munich coup that almost did Hitler in, but even then, a special something watched out for the ex-corporal after his arrest. At his trial in March of 1924, the judge was sympathetic to the Party and so the sentence was light. "Five years for treason," Hitler remarked to his lawyer after hearing the penalty. "I'll be out in less than a year," Hitler chuckled under his breath, "less than a year."

"And Landsberg Prison," his attorney murmured slyly, "what a Godsend!"

Hitler smirked and made sure not to make it too obvious to the throng of courtroom onlookers. Hitler knew the publicity from the trial had more than made up for the failure of his attempted coup that had given the Nazi Party and its leader more that they had dreamt of. "I shall be a figure of Wagnerian proportions," Hitler exclaimed as he waited in the court's outer rooms to be transferred to the prison. "I am now a product and if marketed correctly in the tumult of the Weimar Republic, we can sell our brand to the people." He was speaking to the other men, high Party officials, Joseph Goebbels, Rudolf Hess, and Martin Borman. "We shall be the new barbarians." Hitler was directly his words towards Goebbels. "The old order will fall before us like a house of cards."

"Indeed," he replied, "for we shall learn to divide our opponents, my Fuhrer, just as the Romans did to theirs."

"I shall be the new knight errant," Hitler blustered as he strode about the room, posturing grandly, "come to slay the multi-headed hydra of Judaism, Communism, and Republicanism," he exclaimed. "All I need do is write it down, and like a Grimm brother's folk tale, the German faithful can read and learn of the glorious visions for a Third Reich."

"Yes, yes," Goebbels chimed in, "the time you spend at Landsberg will give you a chance to work out a book."

"A bible for the Party," Borman interjected.

Hitler stopped, turned, and with a wicked grin on his face, said excitedly, "Yes, a bible for the new world order we will achieve."

"Yes," Hess shouted, "a blueprint for the thousand-year Reich!"

Hitler nodded, stamped his feet with glee, and smiled broadly as they waited for the prison transport to come to take Hitler to jail.

SEVEN

Some months later, Hitler sat in his large and well furnished cell writing with only his personal secretary Borman still there, since Hess had already left. After Hitler finished his newest passage, he spoke to his companion, "The Americans are right, Borman," Hitler said as he massaged his tired writing hand. "Exposure, constant exposure of a product will sell anything, even tooth paste." The mirth in Hitler's voice was evident as he continued. "The Americans have taught me how to market a products and so we shall become salesmen for the new Order of the Reich."

Borman nodded and continued writing down every word Hitler was saying in the journal he kept.

"We shall sell ourselves through slogans and the movies," Hitler began confidently as he rose and started to pace about the cell. "These will be the tools for our success, and even though I do love the British," he went on, "it is those Americans, those mongrels of the New World, who can sell anything. How I would love to unite all the Anglo-Saxons, everywhere, but never those bastardized Americans, not them. Yet," Hitler continued as he slapped his hands with glee, "we shall learn from the Americans though for, in the last war, their propaganda against us was outstanding. Outstanding, Borman! Raping nurses and bayoneting babies, indeed," Hitler said, chuckling as he rarely did. "But it played well in the movie houses, and we shall never forget that Martin, never!" Hitler's voice had taken on a visionary tone. He stopped his pacing now and was staring out the cell's window, thinking. Finally, he began, "Today, Germany," and pounded his fist into his hand, unsure of what to say next.

"Tomorrow, the World," Borman interjected.

Hitler turned slowly and looked at his secretary and smiled. "Yes, Borman you're right. Why didn't I think of it!" Hitler cleared his throat and continued, "Today, Germany," and he jabbed his hand dramatically into the air, "tomorrow, the World."

Borman smiled.

"We have it then, Martin," and Hitler leaped with joy, stamping his feet with glee. "There, in five words, five words!" and came back to his desk and sat back down, exhausted from this creative outburst which had created the new Nazi slogan.

Borman waited a moment. Since their publisher was pressing for the finished manuscript, a deadline had to be met so the Party Secretary had to take a chance. Hitler had, once again, been procrastinating on the finished manuscript, so Borman asked, "How goes the book, my Fuhrer?"

"It flows," Hitler said quietly, "like the Rhine, slowly, at times, but every onward, ever onward."

"Good," Borman replied meekly, but pressed further to ensure that Hitler wouldn't delay any longer. "So the fates are with us then, my Fuhrer?"

"No," he replied, his voice sounded hard, the wry smile suddenly gone from his countenance as he turned and looked directly at his Party Secretary. "Choice, Borman, all is choice. Life is choosing. Remember that. We have chosen and so our destiny is before us, but fate is not involved," and he stopped. Rising from the chair again, he put one hand upward and the other near his heart. "We will not be denied our future for we still need living space in Eastern Europe," and Hitler dropped both hands and held them at his waist. He had struck a stance, and like an actor practicing his lines, he sensed he had chosen a formidable pose. "We are the chosen people," he said quite dramatically, "and we will triumph, over all who stand in our way."

As Borman watched, he thought Hitler was a natural actor who could have played Hamlet on the professional stage. "What timing," Borman muttered as he observed Hitler now, but Borman didn't speak up; it wasn't his style to upstage the Party Leader, so like an attentive bit player, he paused and waited for the next cue to come.

"Enough for today, hen," Hitler said. He yawned as he furrowed his brow, and put his hands on his hips. "I shall see you tomorrow, but remember to tell Hess to be ready. He's meeting with those Industrialists and Bankers soon, yes?"

"Yes, my Fuhrer," Borman replied, "Wednesday at 10 AM."

"Bankers hours," the phrase was said with much sarcasm. "Well," Hitler went on, "we need their money to fill our Party's war chests," and abruptly stopped as a thought came to him. When he decided to speak, he spoke slyly, giving a sideways glance to his Secretary. "When the coin in the coffer rings, the soul to Nazism springs."

"Yes, my Fuhrer," Borman chirped back as he grinned broadly at Hitler's pun on the infamous monk Telzel's adage on the selling of indulgences by the Roman Catholic Church. It had been indulgences that had helped spark the German Reformation of 1517.

"Tell Hess," Hitler continued, "to set up a meeting with those capitalists for I want to meet those men of money, face to face," and he winked. "Charm, Borman, it's a gift of mine. Remember, I want to meet with these fat industrialists and bankers myself." Borman noted it in his pad.

"Guard!" Hitler called out loudly. Within a few moments, hurried footsteps sounded and abruptly stopped outside the door as a lock was turned. "Till tomorrow," Hitler said to Borman as the cell door was swung open.

"Good night, my Fuhrer," Borman replied as he rose, but Hitler said nothing. He just stood there, posturing, as Borman left.

After he had gone and the door was sealed, Hitler returned to his desk, reaching for some cigarette. He took one from the pack and lit it. Drawing a deep draft, he inhaled, blew a long stream of smoke, and watched it drift moving slowly out the cell's window. I do like my smokes, but it is a weakness, he thought, then set his chin, so I must test my will on this, I must give these up. I must set a standard. No weaknesses, he concluded, then muttered, "This will be my last one," and, with one hand on his hip, the other holding his final cigarette, he felt better, not so vulnerable. Hitler had gotten used to loneliness, and smoking helped, but tonight its taste distracted him. He had much to do, and little time to do it. What was that the beast had said? Hitler reflected. Three decades to do the job? As he blew another smoke ring, he watched as it gently swirled above his head. "I must be strong," he sputtered, "but there's so little time."

Meanwhile, outside of his cell, a strong fog was coming in and like a cat creeping across the landscape, the mist advanced. Soon it enveloped familiar things about the landscape and within minutes, had wrapped the prison's walls in a thick misty cloak.

As Hitler stared out his window, the bars were becoming slick with beads of water while the air in the room was becoming heavy with humidity making the Party Leader uncomfortable. A haze had formed in his cell too, and seemed to swirl about, creating shadowy movements as if a shape was trying to emerge. It was then he realized there was another presence in the room.

"A trick I use," the vampire said softly as the fog lessened, and it emerged in solid form in front of Hitler.

"Yes," he replied as he flicked his unfinished cigarette away, dropped to one knee, bowed his head and asked, "Lord?"

The beast purred its approval then strode to the desk and saw the manuscript and fingered through the pages for a few moments and said, "The time of your confinement is almost up, little brother, but do not underestimate your opponents." It turned and faced his disciple. "I shall not visit you again for awhile, but you can deal with those industrialists and bankers for they would sell their soul to the Devil for a gold coin." The creature's voice was joyful. "Be charming when you meet them. Be graceful, play a simple fool. Let them think what they want," it growled. As it moved close to Hitler and stood tall over the stooped man, "but you shall snare them all." The vampire's glee was evident as it raised Hitler's head in its hands and stared into the Fuhrer's eyes like a parent instructing a child. "You must choose again. Friends or the goal and in that," it asked, "what are friends?" Before Hitler could reply, the vampire answered its own question. "Tools, just tools," it cooed, "so make use of them, but sacrifice them wisely when the time comes," and dropped its hand from the Hitler's face. "Value these industrialists and bankers, become their ally, and then," raising its voice slightly, the beast cried, "throw them into the fire! Remember," it exclaimed, "our master is not money, not

Germany, not God. God doesn't exist for us! Use these men of wealth as you will use the Pacifists, those dreamers for world peace," it sneered, "those meek romantics who dream of the end of war."

At the vampire's performance, Hitler was spellbound.

"And what of the League of Nations, you may ask?" the thing bellowed as it began to strut like a ballroom dancer about the cell. "What fools they are, for how can they win against our purposeful evil, for without the United States in the League, the old alliance of France and England will not hold against our aggression." Its words were ringing in the Party Leader's ears, striking the cords of his heart, reaching to his very soul. "Remember, little brother, we shall triumph and we must never lose sight of our goal. Has not all I have told you about come true so far?"

"Yes," Hitler replied and then asked, "And the Jews, my Lord?"

"Ah the Jews," the creature smirked. "Does anyone remember the Armenians?"

"No, Lord. The Turks did us a favor there after the war, so you were right."

"Has not that genocide in Armenia only just happened," the vampire mockingly replied, "and yet, how soon the general public forgets those atrocities, for their collective memory is small and their power for forgetting is enormous!"

Hitler nodded.

"The public will not believe what you propose do to the Jews, a race already despised by these good Christian men over the centuries. Spread your lies about the sons of Abraham, sell these lies like you would toothpaste," the beast crooned as it held up Hitler's as yet unfinished book. "We must promote ourselves,

Wolf, with the tools of propaganda," the vampire proclaimed, "so remember, we are purveyors, traveling tinkers, creating a market for our goods," and then it winked. "Be a gracious dealer, do anything, say anything, but lure them all to enlist in our cause of their own free will."

"It shall be so, my Lord, " Hitler answered.

"Good," the vampire replied, "so continue to serve Satan well and 1,000 years of his rule will be established through you," and it pointed a finger at the Fuhrer. "You will be Satan's first instrument," and the creature paused, "but the forces arrayed against us are still strong, but every day we too gain strength. Remember," the vampire continued in a lilting tone, "I will be with you, even unto the destruction of God's people." At that moment, the fog grew thicker and swirled around the beast till only a faint red glow flickered where its eyes were. Within seconds, even that was gone.

The Party Leader went to his cell's window and looked out for a long time but to no avail for he couldn't find the creature in the fog. "I will trust in my master," Hitler murmured and turned from the view and began to pace. When his nervous energy was exhausted, he called out, "Guard!"

Within seconds footsteps resonated again, followed by the sound of the sliding panel on the cell's door. "Yes?" a nervous voice asked.

"I need more supplies." Hitler bellowed. He sounded cranky. While the key was turned and after the door opened, the jailer entered. Nervously, he stood before Hitler who shouted, "Now!"

"Sir," the jailer replied as he clicked his boots together.

"Strong coffee too, I think," Hitler added as he lowered his belligerent tone.

"And cigarettes?" the jailer responded, expecting the usual answer.

"No." The prisoner replied, but there was no anger in his tone now for his playing of the jailer's emotions had worked.

He looked puzzled since this item was among the famous man's constant requests so the jailer asked about another favorite selection. "And chocolate?"

"No." Hitler responded, pleased at the guard's quandary, "just paper and coffee, that is all."

The jailer nodded and left quickly, leaving the door wide open.

Returning to his writing desk, Hitler sat down and opened a side drawer where a box of Swiss chocolates was and eagerly took just one and set it by his writing pad. Next, he pulled out a pack of cigarettes and looked longingly at them and then put them in the dustbin. He did the same for the open pack on the top of the desk as well. "There," he said and pounded his leg for emphasis. "Will, all is will," he muttered. "It is what separates great men from the masses. It is what gives us strength," and he smiled then grabbed his pen and thought, I must write this down, and he began to write furiously. After a few minutes, he was so engaged in his writing that he didn't notice the jailer who had re-entered the room. Quietly, the guard placed the tray with the coffee and paper on it on Hitler's desk and left quietly, not wishing to interrupt the famous man's writings.

While the words flowed from the Hitler's pen, after a few moments, he paused to read what he had just written. "The triumph of will is achieved only by blood and sacrifice. Only those ready to sacrifice can choose the path to the greater glory of the Volk. Only through the will of the Fuhrer is the true will of the Volk expressed. Their will is his will, his will is theirs, and so united, no force on Earth can stop the true people's destiny. Through their will, as expressed by the Fuhrer, the new World Order will be established, the new Reich will rise, and the whole world shall be united." He put his pen aside and muttered "Glorious."

After a few more moments, he took the dark chocolate candy and put it in his mouth. As the first bitter taste sensations swept across his taste buds, he sighed deeply. "How sweet," he murmured, and felt good. After he finished the treat, while the taste of the confectionary still lingered in his mouth, he took up the pen again and began to write more. Time for him had lost its meaning, only the present, only the creative mood he was in was important and that is what he really enjoyed. "How sweet," he mumbled again as he continued to write, "how sweet."

EIGHT

BERLIN, 1933

The two secretaries were working late, again. The others in the office pool had long ago departed the Chancellery building, but the senior typist and her aide had been instructed to remain. They had been rudely informed of this by their section leader, Herr Tappen, near to the office's closing. "The Fuhrer will be staying late," Tappen snapped, the gleam in his eyes apparent, for he was hoping to frustrate the women's evening plans for he was a vile little man, "and you two will remain here."

Liza Mann, the senior of the two women, would have none of the bureaucrat's arrogant attitude in addressing her without the proper use of her title. "Yes, Herr Tappen," she replied, not using his title either. The tone of her voice was soft but conveyed a sense of determination, evidence of a strong will that had aided her in the lean years after the First World War. She had joined the Nazi Party early, and unlike Tappen, was a true Hitler fanatic, and so had major Party connections. This fact was something Tappen knew, but couldn't abide, especially in a woman.

"Yes, Fraulien Mann, the Fuhrer has much to do," Tappen responded, his tone was surly and confrontational, and his usage of her unmarried title was meant to sting.

It's going to be another test of wills, thought the younger woman, Gretchen Schmidt, as she watched Tappen and Mann battle once again. These office contests made Gretchen uncomfortable, and it showed in her facial expression that Tappen immediately picked up on as he gazed suggestively at her. Gretchen detested the man and his looks, but learned to live with both. As long as Liza is here, Gretchen reflected, he can't touch me, but she didn't look at him directly. She was too much of a survivor herself to do that so she kept an outwardly submissive demeanor, for she, like the others in this office, knew the rules. It was something you learned fast, or you didn't stand a chance of making it in post war Germany, especially now that Hitler was Chancellor.

"The Chancellor has ordered another election," Tappan continued as he turned back towards Mann. "He'll need those updated voter registration indexes, and you two," he paused, "will remain until they are done." Like a little rooster, Tappen puffed out his chest, glanced over the rims of his small eyeglasses, and crowed, "Understand."

Gretchen continued to look at the floor but Liza stared right back at Tappan. She had never flinched during the entire interchange, for she was an office veteran, and no living thing would best her in these turf wars.

"Now," Tappen bellowed, "get to it," and when neither woman moved, he turned and started to stride away, a loser in this present skirmish, but as both Mann and he knew, the office war wasn't over. "Tomorrow is another day," he muttered just loud enough to be heard as he slammed the door as he left.

Liza stood unshakable in her silence for she could care less what that little man thought. She knew that today's contest of wills, although small, would add up, and soon she would triumph. Liza had her own schedule and she kept too it, for Liza was a patient woman, skilled in the methods of office warfare.

"Swine," Gretchen uttered now that Tappen was gone.

"Shh," Liza hissed softly as she turned towards the younger woman, "be careful, Kitten," and extended a graceful hand toward Gretchen's face. As her raven black hair fell off to one side, Liza smiled but took back her hand quickly. "Later tonight, yes, but now," and her voice grew firm, "back to work." As the senior typist returned to her desk and began their Herculean task, for Liza, at least, the work was a labor of devotion for she cherished the Nazi cause more than her life. This fact was something the older senior Party members, especially Hitler, counted on, and so gave her domain far beyond what Tappan would have ordinarily allowed. Her desire for Gretchen was something new, nurtured by their infatuation, but lust would have to wait for later, as Liza threw herself into the task of compiling the new voter lists.

The confrontation with Tappen had been shortly after 4 P.M., but it was now near 7 P.M. and growing dark outside. The street lamps were on as the women worked, lost in their task, and they had switched on their desk lamps. Shadows in the large room were increasing while the sun's decreasing light spread out like movie projector's rays with dust particles dancing in the beams. It was just after the wall clock struck 8t P.M., when a particular shadow, larger than the others, made its way across from the doorway and edged closer to where the two secretaries worked. Like a stalking cat, the shadow inched forward, carefully, steadily, silently, in short, powerful movements, always keeping away from the light, and always headed towards Liza's desk. When close to it, as if a pane of glass had been shattered by a rock, a voice broke the women's concentration and asked, "Is he in?"

As if an electric shock had been applied to them, the secretaries bolted upright. Gretchen's breathing stopped briefly as she clutched her breast and Liza, although startled, was able to look in the direction of the voice. Her hands were flat on the desk and one, the left, was trembling unconsciously as a figure eased into her lamp's light. The man was dressed as if he were about to attend a State gala. He wore a black, tailed tuxedo while his evening cape, made of a glossy velvet material, hung flawlessly over his shoulders. His hands, ungloved, were massive as they protruded under the sleeves of his tuxedo, and he stood there erect, like a human obelisk. While Liza stared, he shifted his weight, ever so slightly, in an attempt to control an energy that lay beneath. As he waited for a reply, the strain of controlling himself showed in his countenance.

"Yes," Liza finally said, "the Fuhrer is in." While she studied the dapper man, she noticed his blond hair and those eyes. It was those eyes that triggered recognition in her brain and, immediately, she picked up the phone, pushed a button, paused, and waited for a response.

While this was being done, the man studied her with a jaundiced look, but remained silent. The fierceness in its eyes never lessened and the sense of these women's fear warmed him.

Finally she replied to a voice on the phone. "Yes my Fuhrer, Herr Block is here." She paused, "Yes, I will show him in," then another pause, "yes, immediately." As Liza rose, she put the phone down and said in a polite manner, "This way, Herr Block." When they arrived at the Chancellor's door, she knocked, waited, then opened it and motioned Herr Block past. As he went by, she could feel his energy, and it made her swoon.

Once he was inside, she closed the door and went back to her desk.

"Unbelievable," Gretchen said as she came over to Liza's desk. "So that is the mysterious Herr Block you've whispered about to me in bed."

"Yes," Liza replied, her voice racing with excitement. "He's a close and old friend of the Fuhrer's that I've met only a few times."

Gretchen, an ambitious woman, seemed enthralled as she waited for Liza to continue about Herr Block.

"The first time," she went on, hesitated and continued, "was back in 1923 just before the failed coup in Munich. He came to the Party Office several times, at night," and she looked at Gretchen who now sat perched on the desk's edge, seductively. "I was told he had immediate entrance to the Fuhrer, at any time."

"Really." The young woman sounded fascinated. "Why?"

"Old Comrades," she replied as she looked lovingly into the Gretchen's face for she had drawn closer. "They go back to the Great War." Liza restrained herself from her passion for it was instinctive for her to do so, especially nurtured by her personal lifestyle. "Careful," and she pointed a finger at Gretchen and wagged it slowly. "Too much curiosity killed the pussy cat," and paused, looked around quickly and added, "No more," and reached out and touched her lover's hand.

"Hmm," Gretchen muttered as she backed off from the desk for she had been rebuffed, but took it in stride. Once at her desk she sputtered, just loud enough for Liza to hear, "Bitch."

She smiled back, engagingly and said, "Whore."

Gretchen laughed at their ritual exchange, then looked again at the many papers on her desk, and sputtered. "But first, lists, lists,

lists. Cross Schmidt with party affiliation, Schindler with voter registration, Snyder with," and stopped and tilted her head and said, "but then there's Herr Block."

"Get a hold," Liza countered, but not too angrily.

"It will be hard to forget Herr Block," Gretchen sighed and coyly added, "what a figure," and blew a kiss towards Liza, after which, muttered, "but who needs men."

While the two secretaries returned to their work, meantime in the Chancellor's office, Hitler had remained seated until the door was fully closed. After that, the disciple rose quickly, moved from behind his desk, knelt with bowed head and said, "Lord."

"Rise," Block commanded as he approached. The fear in the Chancellor's face, the awe in his eyes, pleased the beast as it tossed out a question. "This election, will we win it?"

"It will be close Lord," Hitler responded, "but, yes, we can for we are in charge of the election's machinery now," and the Chancellor held up some of the papers on his desk. "We have access to all the voter information forms." Hitler's voice was confident as he continued, "The flock is ours for the taking."

"And like the wolf," the beast countered expecting a reply.

"We will destroy this putrid Weimar Republic," Hitler responded. "The names on the lists are the key, for with them we can swing enough voters to our side, if we apply pressure. We only need a simple majority to rule the Reichstag, Lord, so I will set Rohm's brown-shirted savages on the undecided voters. The streets will run red with their blood."

"Yes," the beast purred, "but you must deal with Rohm after that."

"I understand, Lord," Hitler answered.

"You have done well, little brother," the vampire continued, his tone expressed his satisfaction, "but I have a twist for our plan," and the creature chuckled before it went on. "A fire, I think, nothing like a good fire, yes," and the beast was pointing out the window towards a government building. "The Reichstag should do nicely."

Instantly, Hitler understood. "Brilliant, Lord,, but who should we blame for the destruction?"

"The Communists." It was said flippantly.

"Lord?" the Chancellor asked.

The beast scrutinized his disciple before answering. "We'll save the Jews for a bit," and Block lip's curled wickedly. "No, the Communists are the more convenient opponent this time. Besides, I have recruited a lunatic, a Dutchman, who will do the job for us. The fool thinks that such a fire in the Reichstag will help to stop your Party's election," and the vampire pointed a finger at the Chancellor, "so we'll use another fool to do the Devil's work." Hitler drew back at this insinuation on his own mental status, but the vampire didn't care. "The insane are quite useful to us Wolf, never forget that, so use them wisely," and the vampire hesitated on purpose, "like you do Hess and Rohm."

"Yes Lord," Hitler responded carefully, trying to hide some of his petulance.

"Come," and the beast motioned for Hitler to draw closer, "let me explain." After the vampire put his arm around his pupil and drew him even nearer, "This will be a most useful exercise for you to learn from for it's quite simple really." While the creature continued to talk, they gazed across the street towards the Reichstag as the beast explained how its plan would work to ensure a Nazi electoral victory.

After the fire was set, the Reichstag burned, and Hitler went on national radio and gave an emotional speech to the nation, in which he called for blood and victory against the forces set upon the destruction of the Reich. At its conclusion, he laid the blame directly on the Communists. "These Bolsheviks conspire to destroy our property, our freedom and our Reich," he bellowed into the microphone. "These plotters sneak about to destroy Germany, and we alone, the National Socialists stand up to the Red Menace." He paused. "We, alone, stand for German freedom," Hitler continued on confidently, "and we, alone, defend the Fatherland!" He stopped again briefly, gathered a deep breath and spoke forcefully into the microphone, the new slogan he had written, "So if you want your country to go Bolshevik, vote Communist, but if you want to remain free Germans, vote Nazi!"

"What a performance," Goebbels exclaimed off mike to Hess as a large applause broke out in the room from the invited spectators. They had been gathered to hear Hitler's address and were now responding loudly.

"Indeed," Hess shouted as he clapped even louder, "indeed."

Standing further back, Borman was clapping too, a wide smile on his face.

Yet, the German electorate didn't give the Nazis a clear parliamentary majority in the election. Consequently, a coalition government had to be made, and once the Nazi seduced a minority party to join in a coalition of their two parties, under the Weimar Republic's constitution, now having a 51% of the representation in the Reichstag, these two parties were the elected government. It was under that provision of the Weimar Republic's constitution that the forces of evil became legitimatized and, by July, The Enabling Act had been passed in the Reichstag. Under this new law, Germany became a single party state and all other political parties were declared illegal. As a result, democracy was legislatively ended in Germany and totalitarianism became the order of the day. Any who resisted the new single party state could be legally and systematically eliminated as traitors to the official government and so a reign of terror began under the German Robespierre, Hitler.

With the passage of this law, at the private celebration organized by Goebbels, the new Reich Minister of Propaganda, Hitler was in a jubilant frame of mind. Hess and Borman were there as were Himmler and Rohm, who sat on opposite ends of the room. Goring was the last to arrive, and after several minutes of small talk, Goebbels' wife and the few women in attendance withdrew, after leaving some drinks and appetizers on the coffee table.

"We've done it," the Fuhrer exclaimed as he slapped his knee confidently. He was sitting in a wingback chair with his comrades facing him in a semicircle. Presently, he took up a fluted glass and raised the Bavarian crystal high. "Gentlemen," he stated as the others scrambled to get theirs, then Hitler stood. Immediately, the others followed suit.

"Puppets," Borman muttered as he looked around sheepishly being the last one to rise.

"To the Third Reich!" Hitler exclaimed.

"To the Reich," the others chorused in as they raised their glasses and sipped. Following the toast, Hitler, a wide smile on his face, sat down, followed by the others.

"What of the Jews, my Fuhrer?" It was Himmler, the head of the State Security Police, the dreaded SS, who spoke.

"Yes," Hitler quipped, "what of them?"

"We must bring them to a reckoning, my Fuhrer."

"We shall, we shall, Henrich, but first," Hitler hesitated, "some diversion." His remark caused a small ripple of laughter among the guests, for it was rare for Hitler to joke, but today, today was a day of joy for the Fuhrer.

"My Fuhrer," Himmler responded as the laughter subsided.

Hitler cut him off playfully. "Patience, Henrich, patience," and Hitler waved his hand in a kindly way. "We must be methodical, yes, so, let us burn a few books in public places first."

"A rally, my Fuhrer," Goebbels broke in. "What a great idea."

"Yes, Joseph, for I have in mind many grand rallies across the entire Reich. Let us rid ourselves of those stinking books. Those works of Freud, Einstein, Hemingway, Keller, and Remarque."

"And Thomas Mann too, my Fuhrer." It was Hess speaking excitedly now.

"Yes," the Fuhrer answered. "We shall bask in the firelight as they burn. We shall empty the libraries, the private collections and all the archives. We shall burn all we can find. It will be a mid-summer night's dream." Hitler was playing to Hess, a mystic, but still useful to Hitler so, on occasion, Hitler would heighten Hess's dreams, but today, Hitler had more than just dreams in mind. "Fires are useful, they make for wonderful images in the people's minds," and he glanced over towards Goebbels, "especially when well-lit in the evening's darkness."

"Night rallies," Goebbels blurted out for he had instantly picked up on Hitler's inspiration. "Yes," Goebbels shouted with glee, "they will have such a good effect, my Fuhrer. The flames will enhance the camera's view as they dance across the movie screens in a ballet of purification. It will be a pagan rite of spring."

"Then night rallies it shall be," and Hitler thumped his leg. "Think of them," and he looked around the room for he was working the gathering. "Huge masses of the Volk, banners, music, fire, a festival of savagery whose flickering images will play well on the newsreels," and he glanced at Hess. "We shall reach into every cinema house in Germany, and we will be on every screen, and in all the beer halls."

Hess was nodding like a bobble headed doll.

"Sounds like you two are Hollywood directors pitching a film," Goring sputtered as he reached for an appetizer.

"Quite so," Hitler snapped as he smirked at Goring, but didn't reprimand him for his impertinence.

"We will have live broadcasts too," Hitler ranted, "and the airwaves will echo with your message, Josef, into every house in Germany."

"Indeed," Goebbels clamored. "We can use the radio as it has never been used before," the flush of inspiration taking hold even more. "We shall penetrate into every household in Germany, and your broadcasts of the glorious triumph of Aryanism will electrify the Reich, my Fuhrer."

Hitler smiled wickedly.

"Why," Hess murmured, "we can even reach Austria with our transmitters."

"My thoughts exactly," Hitler replied as he slyly glanced around and saw the smiles of his companions growing, for they all knew of Hitler's desire to unite Germany with Austria.

However, during most of this exchange, Himmler had remained politely silent, but now decided to interject his thoughts on some other issues for the new Reich. "What of Dachau, my Fuhrer? When shall we begin?"

"You have your legislation, Henrich," Hitler replied with a small grimace as he looked at the sober faced Himmler. "The Enabling Act," Hitler continued as he quickly shifted his jubilant mood to a more serious one, "allows you to set up the camp and from this process, the Reich will be purged by your SS men."

The Fuhrer's voice was taking on a mystic quality as he stared above the heads of his followers for he had begun his testing of Himmler and Rohm. "Our blood will be made clean by your SS men in that killing place."

"Yes, my Fuhrer," Himmler replied as he pushed his real motive with Hitler, "but what shall be the role of the SS after that?"

Damn, that SS pup, Rohm, the head of the Sturmabteilung, the infamous Brown Shirts, the paramilitary arm of the Nazi Party, fumed as he sat up. He now was prepared to do battle with Himmler. "Not much," Rohm snarled like a fierce attack dog rising to defend its territory, "if you ask me."

They've started, Borman thought, then looked at Hitler to see what he might have in store this time by provoking these two rivals.

"Gentlemen," Hitler replied as he took up his glass for he knew the final life and death duel between Rohm's and Himmler's organizations role in the new Reich was fast approaching, yet, Hitler wanted to delay it some just now, so he deflected Himmler's request by stating, "Another toast is in order, gentlemen, for in the old and decadent Germany, the Kaiser's Imperial Navy used to have a saying, remember?"

Most nodded, but Goring moaned and looked lazily over at Hess and snidely muttered a single word, "Anglophile."

Hess whose love of the British was well known, caught Goring's gesture and glared back. "Swine," he sputtered, but Goring countered with just a sly smile.

"Today," Hitler continued, deciding to ignore Goring and Hess' childishness, "I propose to change the meaning of that old toast. Today, I propose that we shall all, together, help to purify

Europe," and looked slowly about and said, "and to that end, gentleman, I give you, 'To our Day!'"

Instantly, those gathered raised their glasses and chimed in with, "Here, here." After the toast, but before Himmler could speak anew, Hitler looked at Borman and asked, "What of the Hitler Youth, Martin? How goes it?"

"The legislation is prepared, my Fuhrer," Borman quickly replied, "and within days, it shall be passed and implemented."

"Good, good," Hitler replied in a satisfied tone. "Yes, gentlemen we shall imitate the ancient Greeks by taking our young and indoctrinating them, so that the child will become the man." He looked at Himmler. "It is the youth of the Reich that holds the key to our 1,000 year survival, for the Aryan nation is founded on several bedrocks, and that shall be one." Hitler now looked at Goebbels. "We shall burn books by the thousands which will give the young a show, a night of pageantry, of purposeful destruction. All impressionable children need such nights," Hitler cooed as he worked his magic on his intimate followers. "We shall harness the youth of Germany to the Aryan Nation by these rallies, and the Hitler Youth will give us a faithful horde of dedicated recruits," Hitler ranted. "These youth with turn into men, ready to defend the Fatherland, without hesitation," and he slapped his fist into his right hand, "and without the old Christian morality to hold them back from service to the Fatherland."

"A new Sparta." It was Rohm speaking, for it was time, he judged to speak again. "Glorious, my Fuhrer, glorious," but Rohm was staring at Himmler. "A new host, the peoples' militia, that is what my Brown Shirts are," Rohm hissed confidently, "something truly glorious."

"No, it shall not be egalitarian," Himmler snapped as if a gauntlet had been thrown down. "No," he continued firmly, "our new Order must be based on a proper elite," the SS headmaster pontificated, "and like a warrior priesthood, the SS will be dedicated to our lord, the Fuhrer. The SS," Himmler exclaimed, "will be hardened disciples, not a mob," and he glared at Rohm, "not an undisciplined Volk's militia, like the Brown Shirts."

Borman watched with keen intent as this contest between the leaders of the SS and the Brown Shirts for Borman knew Hitler had manipulated the conversation towards it. It was a dangerous game Hitler was playing, Borman knew, but it needed to be done, especially if the Army, now being enlarged despite the Treaty of Versailles, was to be brought under the control of the Chancellor. In anticipation, Borman waited to see who would speak next.

"We are all dedicated to the Fuhrer, Reichminister," Rohm countered, his words like a thunderbolt resonated in the room. In reaction, Himmler braced himself and grabbed the armrests of his chair. "My Fuhrer," Rohm was standing, "the Brown Shirts have always stood ready to march, to fill the streets with your faithful storm troopers. We have been there with you from the beginning, from the earliest of days, from Munich in 1923, " and Rohm turned and looked at Hitler. The Fuhrer had placed his arms on the sides of his seat and was watching intently, but spoke not a word. Seeing this, Rohm turned and faced Himmler and shouted, "We are not some black booted, pretty boys in fancy uniforms who squawk like frightened women at the sight of blood. We, the Brown Shirts, are the true barbarians, not the SS. We, my boys, the SA, are held to our Fuhrer by a blood bond that only death can destroy," and Rohm paused dramatically, but seemed ready to pounce on Himmler.

He looked flushed now, for at heart he was a meek man, as Hitler knew, and didn't like confrontation, especially ones with Rohm. Hitler also knew, that Himmler was just the kind of sly conspirator who could be useful in eliminating threats to the Fuhrer's power, especially from street thugs like Rohm. Finally, Hitler knew that the old officers corps of the Regular Army, mostly Prussians, detested Rohm and his men and viewed the SA as a threat to an expanding Regular Army.

"We are the Volks Army," Rohm continued as he turned and again looked at Hitler, "and all tremble before us, for none will stand in our way," and then Rohm beat his chest. "In the new Reich, the People's Army of the SA will push aside all enemies for the glory of the Fuhrer for we, the SA are the iron fist of the Party." Rohm turned now and pointed at Himmler, "You and your kind are only policemen." The last word was said with such a disdain that it made even Hess flinch.

Meanwhile, Borman watched and waited.

"My Fuhrer," Rohm continued as he turned and held out his two hands and curled them into fists, "the SA stands ready to take over the role of the Army in the new Reich, and you, my Fuhrer, only have to say the word, and it shall be so."

"What of those Prussian Junkers?" Goring blurted out, attempting to interject his views into this confrontation on the Reich's new military, especially wondering how it would affect his own branch of the service, the air service, the expanding Luftwaffe.

"We shall destroy the officer class," Rohm screamed, "and we shall replace them all. We need no aristocrats in the Volkstrum. We are the Reich's true warriors. It was something we learned in the Great War, and we shall not be stabbed in the back again by those vermin in the Army." Hitler was finally smiling, but knew enough to let Rohm finish. "In the new order, my boys, the SA leads the way and we shall smash all before us," and he glance around the room slowly adding, "all."

"There will be plenty of smashing to do, I promise you, Ernst," Hitler said as the Alpha male in the room. "We all shall delight too in the crushing of the old, of the destruction of the petty bourgeoisie, of international Jewry, of the decadent western culture, and of the Communists." Hitler raised his right hand and pointed at Rohm. "We shall bathe in the blood of our enemies, and so the SA still leads, my old friend," and Hitler lingered a moment, "but the Brown Shirts and the SS each have vital roles to play in the new Reich, so, Ernst prepare your legions, but," Hitler added quietly, "we will have to deal with the Army and those Prussian Junkers carefully," and winked at his old comrade from the streets. "Remember, keep your enemies close," and Hitler pounded his knee violently, "and then strike hard!"

Rohm thinking he had triumphed turned and looked towards Himmler, gave him a wicked smile, and sat down.

Himmler, a true survivor and wily conspirator, knew enough not to say anything at this point and just sat there, quietly.

If looks could kill, Himmler is a dead man, Borman pondered as he glanced at Rohm, whose triumphant look indicated his intent towards the head of the SS.

"Henrich," Hitler began in a long, drawn out tone, "build your penitentiary at Dachau and put a motto over the front gate, for all to see as they enter. Use this, 'And work shall make you free,'" then, like the actor he was, Hitler paused. "We shall gather in the sheaves, yes, the harvest will be brought to us for all who resist, first the Communists, then the labor unions, then the Catholics, and then, of course, the Jews, all will be sent to you, Henrich, and none will escape your scythe. Learn to kill at Dachau," and

Hitler chuckled. "Do it methodically and with Aryan precision. Be a good jailer," and his tone was like a schoolmaster's. "Train your men and once killing has become a habit, once death has become normal, customary, then, "and he shook his finger, "they'll be ready," and Himmler nodded. "Now," the Fuhrer said gently, "let us not bicker like children, for we have man's work to do," and he held his arms wide open. The stance reminded Borman of Christ, as if Hitler were giving the Sermon on the Mount. "The meek must be destroyed," Hitler said calmly, "and from that destruction, we shall build a new order, but remember, time waits for no one." After saying that, Hitler reached for his glass and held it up. "To the greater glory of the Aryan Nation."

"To the greater glory of the Aryan nation!" the others called out and then all drank their full measure.

Following this toast, Borman looked about, first at Rohm, and then at Himmler, and then at the Fuhrer. I wonder what he's planning? Borman asked himself.

Hitler, whose gaze caught everything in a small group, noticed Borman's expression, and when their eyes met, the Fuhrer raised an eyebrow and put his middle, index finger to his nose. Borman saw the obscene gesture and the mirth upon the Fuhrer's face and blurted out, "Somebody's screwed."

"What's that you said?" Goring asked having overheard Borman's muttering.

"Oh, nothing," he answered, "just thinking out loud." As he hid his smile, Borman thought, Wonder which one it is?

NINE

"The Royal Air Force is the modern bulwark of England," the Air Marshall said as he was about to finish his address to Parliament sitting in judgment of whether or not to add new funding for the RAF. "And in the days of sail," he continued, "the fate of the nation depended on English hearts of oak, but today," he went on and amid the mutterings of "Here, here," from members of the Prime Minister's party, "but today, enemy air fleets can fly over our warships and so our precious isles must be prepared to meet the foe in the air, as well as on the sea."

"Here, here," the Prime Minister's loyalists cried out loudly, but not the members of the Opposition who sat across the way, most of whom just sat there, unmoved as of yet. Parliament's debates had reached a crucial stage and the RAF Commander had been brought in to help sway today's vote by the Prime Minister.

"We need to keep the Navy formidable, as always," the Air Marshall said firmly, "but the times, honorable members, decree to us that we must look to the skies, as well, for our protection. Today, long range bombers can fly to strike at London, Birmingham and Manchester, which is something the Italians have demonstrated with their aerial displays of recent demonstration," He paused. "Consequently, if we do not heed this lesson by the Italians, if we do not prepare now, in the future, the skies over England will rain death upon us all."

"Go on," the Prime Minister muttered softly to the Air Marshall, "go on!" for the Prime Minister could see some backbenchers across the way nodding their heads.

"You, honorable members," the Air Marshall pleaded, "must be men of courage and vision. You must vote yes for the increased funds adequate to keep the Royal Air Force up to date. If you do so," and he raised his arm as he raised his voice, "our fighters will rise up as a swarm of spitfires to meet the foe, whomever they may be." He glanced around the chamber. "If an attack comes, the fight must take place not over the homes and factories of our nation, no, this fight must be fought over the Channel. It is there, away from our sacred shores that we must face the foe."

A rippling of applause rose in the chamber and resonated from the Opposition's side of the House of Commons.

"As a product of increasing the RAF's funding, our planes shall engage the enemy's Armada over the Channel," the Air Marshall exclaimed, "with the same fortitude that our ancestors displayed under Good Queen Bess!" His words brought about another round of applause for all the members viewed Elizabeth the First as good. "A new Saint Crispin's Day is coming, gentlemen," he thundered as he swept his arms outward, "and how shall we respond?" and he let the question hang, but only for a few precious moments. "Will we be brave?" he continued. "Will we be a band of brothers?" and he hesitated, "Will we keep England safe by not only increasing our fighter planes, but also our long range bombers?" His last statement echoed in the House. "The time is now for members of this House to decide," the Marshall concluded in a grand climax. "The moment is here," and he pointed with his right hand to the sky, "the choice is yours," and like a conductor who signaled for a final crescendo, the Marshall brought his ending on, "We must never slacken," he proclaimed, as the applause began again. "So I say to you, like Nelson at Trafalgar when he signaled the fleet," and the Air Marshall leaned forward, with both hands on rail, "England expects every man to do his duty!"

With his concluding statement, a wild applause sounded in the chamber with some members of the Prime Minister's party on their feet, some cheering, but not the Opposition members on the other side of the chamber. After the Marshall sat down, he leaned over to his aide, Major Dudley, and said. "Years of pacifist sentiment," and the Marshall nodded towards several members of the Opposition's leadership not clapping. "They're honorable men, Major, but misguided by that sly fox, Hitler."

"True, Sir," Dudley replied, "but using Nelson's quote was a good touch."

"Quite," the Air Marshall replied with a wink. "They're principled men, Dudley, so we'll see if my signal struck a similar cord with some of their backbenchers. The World's become a perilous place and our little Austrian paper hanger will ditch the Versailles provisions as soon as he can, mark my words on that Major, so prudent men have to arm themselves. I just hope enough of them see that," but before Dudley could reply, an Opposition member rose and was recognized by the House's Speaker.

"Mr. Speaker," Mr. Kent began earnestly, "I appreciate the Air Marshall's wish to defend our wives and our homes, but I question how increasing the bomber fleet will do that," and Kent paused. "Are not bombers offensive in nature," he asked, "and so designed to strike the enemy in their homes?"

"Aye," a few dozen of Kent's supporters shouted encouragingly.

"Will not increasing the RAF's bombers," he stated in a practiced oratorical style, "only encouraging our continental neighbors to increase their air forces?" and he paused, again. Within a flash though, he pressed on. "Will not this buildup begin a new arms race?" and Kent was looking directly at the Prime Minister who was sitting near the Air Marshall. "Have we learned nothing from the tragedy which led to the start of war in 1914?" Kent asked then raised his arms dramatically as a thunderous round of "Here, here," sounded from his side of the House. As Kent stood there, basking in the approval of his members, it was in his long dramatic pause that he made a mistake.

"Mr. Speaker," the Prime Minister screamed, leaping to his feet, "Mr. Speaker."

The Speaker nodded recognition, and Mr. Kent knew he had been outmaneuvered. He blushed a bit, then sat down, reluctantly.

"Members of Parliament," the Government's leader bellowed, "the honorable member has a good point about the Great War and its mistakes, but we have debated that before," and the Prime Minister waved an arm in the air for emphasis. "That is why the Government has presented this present bill to the House in two parts, so let us first vote on the bomber funding, and then on the fighters, but," he said dramatically, "let us not dialogue any more about the nature of war for the time for debate on the RAF increased funding in light of German military build up is over. Now, gentlemen," the Minister thundered, "since the Air Marshall has so eloquently challenged us," and the Prime Minister swept his arm towards the RAF's commander, "we must do our duty, and vote, now, on each of these provisions. Therefore, Mr. Speaker I ask that the present discussion be ended and I hereby call the Question."

"I second that, Mr. Speaker," a member of the Prime Minister's party shouted on cue as he rose to his feet.

When Mr. Kent made no objection from his side of the chamber, the House Speaker called out, "All those in favor of Calling the Question answer, 'Yea,' and the hall resounded with Yeas. "And those opposed?" the Speaker continued, and the Nays responded loudly. Making his decision quickly, the Speaker replied, "The Yeas have it."

Immediately, Kent stood as a loud chorus of angry voices sounded in opposition to the Speaker's ruling. "Mr. Speaker," Kent bellowed, "I call for a Roll Call vote on the questions of funding Bomber Command and increased funding for fighter planes."

"Quiet in the House," the Speaker commanded, but few obeyed. "Order I say," and he rapped his gavel and called out again, "Quiet in the House!" With that, most of the members began to settle down. "The vote," the Speaker said, "on Calling the Question has passed, and this Chair recognizes that a Roll Call Vote on the provisions has been granted as a matter of privilege. Now," and he looked at the House Secretary seated at a table below the Speaker's chair, "Mr. Secretary, please read the first proposed provision and begin the call of the role for each member to vote."

"Here we go," the Air Marshall muttered to no one in particular and while the House had its lengthy vote, as ruled by a Roll Call, he sat back and waited. Once the votes had been tabulated, it was given to the Speaker, who announced that, by a narrow margin, the House had rejected increased funding for the bombers. Amid some boos, he called for order and for the vote on the second provision to take place. Once again the members voted, the votes were counted, and the resulted were handed to the Speaker. By the same narrow margin, the Speaker announced that the House had approved the increased funds for more fighters.

"Well," the Prime Minister said as he turned towards the Air Marshall while a round of a general applause circulated in the chamber, "it's not all we hoped for, but at least you've got your fighters."

"Yes, Prime Minister," the Marshall said firmly, "and England will not want for a horse now."

"I agree," the Prime Minister replied as he extended his hand, "we've done a good service to the nation today."

"We have indeed," the Air Marshall answered, "we have indeed."

"Well," the Minister responded, "I'll let you go then for the hour is growing late."

"Thank you Mr. Prime Minister," the Air Marshall replied as they shook hands, "I will report to your office tomorrow afternoon." Following this, the Marshall turned, and with his aide, Major Dudley, started to make their way out of the House chamber, never noticing the blond German Military Attaché who had been observing the Parliamentary debates from the Visitors Gallery.

During the ride home, the Air Marshall was in a jovial mood. "Never truly get what you want Dudley," he remarked in the back seat of the car. "That's the problem with our democracy. Now," the Air Marshall chirped, "El Duce and Herr Hitler, they know how to stack'em and win, that's for sure."

"Sir," Dudley's voice showed his surprise, "did I hear you correctly?"

"Oh never fear," the Marshall responded, "I don't share our future King's sympathy for the Fritz's and the Ities, but the Prince of Wales could get burned with his infatuation with those two," and let out a sigh. "I do get frustrated with our legislative slowness though," he continued. "Rearmament is a necessary evil. Fighting fire with fire is a dangerous game to be sure, but we must do it too, Dudley." The Marshall's voice had a sad timbre Dudley noticed which was evident as the Marshal went on. "These fascists in Germany and Italy are bullies and they live for war so we have to be ready to face them down, even if it means a new war." It was then the Air Marshall noticed that Dudley's left arm was twitching. "Now lad," the Marshall said calmly, "don't upset yourself by this."

"Sorry," his Aide replied nervously, "still get the shakes sometimes. They come and go, but the Flight Surgeon says I'm getting better."

The Air Marshall reached out a hand and put it on his Aide's shoulder. "Yes, lad, I know. There, there, now," and he left his hand lay upon Dudley in a fatherly way as they rode along now in silence. The Marshall had a reputation for his compassion and he had surrounded himself with veterans of the former Royal Flying Corps, many of whom had stages of what the doctors called "shell shock," like Dudley. Since the death of the Air Marshall's only son on a reconnaissance flight in November of 1918, the Marshall had dedicated himself to two objectives. First was the future defense of England by airplanes and the second was to helping veterans. When he had been chosen First Air Marshall, he landed in a position where he tried to carry out both.

After the car came to a stop in the driveway of the Marshall's residence, and while they going up the steps, he said, "Get me that file on that new German military attaché, what's his name?"

"Lossberg, Sir."

"Yes - the tall Aryan one I believe," the Air Marshall said, a tad out of breath. "Should make for interesting bed time reading." Once inside, he continued, "Send the file up as soon as you can."

"Sir," Dudley responded, "I'll bring it up."

The Air Marshall stopped, turned, slightly out of breath, again. "No, Major, you get some rest. I'll ring Delaney for it. Till breakfast then."

"Yes," Major Dudley answered. "Good night, your Lordship."

"Good night, Dudley."

When the Major got to his first floor office, he took out his file key and opened a tall cabinet by the wall. As he began leafing through the files, when he got to the one he wanted, removed it, just as a knock sounded at the open door.

"Sir," it was Lieutenant Delaney speaking.

"Ah, Delaney," Dudley said as he crossed over and handed Delaney the file. "Tell his Lordship that the photo of Lossberg hasn't yet arrived, we've just his vital stats in here. There's also a Military Intelligence report from our operatives in Berlin."

"Very good, Sir," and Delaney paused. "Oh," he added gently, "his Lordship wanted me to inform you that Flight Surgeon McDougall is on call tonight."

Dudley looked tired.

"We all get'em, Major," Delaney continued, "there's no shame," then he saluted, and left.

Dudley looked at his hands. They looked sweaty and, as he undid his tunic's top button, he turned and headed for his private quarters. When he got there, he looked at the mantel clock, it read 10:33 PM., and so he went over to the shades and pulled them up tight. Sometimes their rattling by the wind sounded like the zip of incoming artillery from the war. The rattling sound might send him into such a fright that he could dive under his bed, shaking and sobbing. Doctor McDougall had been helping Dudley fight the triggers for his Shell Shock. He had advised Dudley to pull the shades up tight every night so, after doing this tonight, went to his bed stand, turned on a light, and sat down in a leather chair that faced the window. While he gazed up, and like a mariner would look for a familiar star reference, he thought of what the Flight Surgeon had told him once. "Pick a star, Major, and use it as a focal point when you get stressed. From that concentration, it will let you find a measure of serenity." Consequently, on a night when Dudley was fighting the shakes, such as tonight, he would focus on a familiar star, trying to fight off the shakes. After a while, he would usually feel tired and could then let go. Tonight, as he did this, he let go and drifted off to sleep.

In the meantime, Lieutenant Delaney, as he headed off, was battling his own stark memories tonight. Seeing Major Dudley had started the Lieutenant thinking of his dead friend, Major Sean Stoker, and especially of Sergeant Smithe's wild account of the failed trench raid. "After our rough encounter before we got to the church with that tall, red eyed blond German, Major Stoker knew the raid was a bust, so he ordered us back, told me to take lead and they'd follow. I was out there a ways, when I heard gun shots from inside the church," Smithe said, his eyes flaring with fear, "but I didn't go back, figuring the lads had been jumped again, and were done for."

As a consequence, Delaney had gone out, without orders, to the church. What he found there was horrified him. There were four corpses, one headless, the other two mangled and withered. Stoker's body was propped up against the wall, but Delaney didn't find the German Smithe said they had captured. After Delaney returned with Stoker's body, without encountering any Germans, the Colonel didn't reprimand the Lieutenant for his unauthorized sortie. Instead, the Colonel recommended Delaney for a Distinguished Service Cross in the recovery of Stoker's body.

Following the Armistice, Delaney stayed in the Second Battalion, but eventually asked for a transfer to the air service in 1919. His war record had impressed the Air Chief who took the Lieutenant on as one of his aides because he reminded the Air Chief of his own dead son. In the subsequent post war years, Delaney and the Air Chief had grown close and Delaney had told many a story about Major Stoker, especially the incident at the church. He also related Stoker's concerns about that blond German that and that seemed to interest the Air Chief the most. After the war, the First Air Marshall was able to help locate Stoker's remains that had been hastily buried in Flanders Fields, and had the body returned for interment on the family's Northern Ireland estate. The Marshall even got the Lieutenant the duty of accompanying the body home, and as a result, his gratitude to the Marshall was even more profound.

Tonight, these memories raced in Delaney's head while he made his way towards the upper bedroom suite. When he got to the door, he knocked loudly and with that his recollections vanished. Since he had permission to do so at anytime, he entered. The Marshall was seated in the large window bay, lazily looking out, and by his side were several files. In his hand, he held a book, which Delaney knew, was the Marshal's Bible and had been with him since his service in France. "Sir," Delaney said softly as he crossed over, "here is the additional file you requested."

"Quite," the Marshall said, his voice sounded maudlin as he put the Bible down.

"Don't forget your medicine Sir," Delaney counseled as he glanced over by the bed stand and saw the full glass of water and pill case nearby.

"Yes, thank you. Rest assured," the Air Marshal continued with a wave of his hand, "I'll take it directly."

"Will that be all then, Sir?"

"No," and he motioned towards a chair, "sit, please." The Lieutenant was often asked to do this especially if it had been a hard day, or if the memories of the Marshall's wife, who had passed two years ago, came back to haunt. The Marshall looked at the Lossberg file and said, "You've seen this Lossberg chap then?"

"Yes, your Lordship, I have. The last time was after I delivered your invitation for the Air Review at the German Embassy and gave it to Lossberg. He's a fine specimen. Just the image of the new man Hitler wishes to create. Tall, muscular, and blond."

"Hmm," the Marshall answered as he scratched his chin thoughtfully, "seems these Aryan types fit a pattern."

"Yes, your Lordship they do," and Delaney hesitated, "but this one's a bit different though."

"How's that?" the Marshall asked inquisitively as he glanced up.

"Have a queer feeling, after meeting this German Attaché," Delaney continued, "for I believe Major Stoker may have encountered this Lossberg too."

"When was that, Lieutenant?"

"1918," he remarked nervously. "We had reports of a big blond German trench raider before the Major's fateful raid."

"Really?" the Air Marshall replied, "but Lossberg's too young to have been in France." The Marshall tapped the file. "According to that man's birth date, he was a child in 1918."

"I know, Sir, that's what I can't figure out, but when I saw Lossberg at the German embassy, he seems to fit the description of that blond bloke we encountered in France. It was something about the man's eyes, at least that's what's Major Stoker told me was in the field reports of those who encountered the German." Delaney stopped. He drew a measured breath and decided to continue. "The Major hinted to me, too, that it might be the same bloke who was trying to stir up trouble in the Balkans before the war."

"Oh yes," the First Marshall said with an air of knowledge. "I knew Stoker before the war, when he served in Military Intelligence in the Balkans. Dedicated chap," and the Marshall pointed at a file on the seat marked, 'Top Secret.' "Interesting reading that, especially the parts on The Black Hand that Stoker was trying to deal with."

"I didn't know you knew of that group," Delaney remarked in some amazement.

"Quite," the Air Marshall responded, a wry smile on his face. "Well, there are things about me, Lieutenant, which I do try and hide, but once Lossberg was assigned to London, I had several prewar files sent over from the Foreign Office. Quite extraordinary reading!" and the Air Marshall paused and took a deep breath. "At times I wonder if God has abandoned us," the Marshall said as he shook his head. "These events in Germany under Hitler are deeply troubling," but the Lieutenant made no comment. "Do you read the Bible, Lieutenant?" the Air Marshall asked.

"I use to, Sir."

Well," he went on, "at times I feel like Job in the Old Testament, plagued by troubles and calamities all round, so we'll just have to watch this Lossberg closely then, that's for sure."

"Yes, your Lordship."

"Good," the Air Marshall said, "so I'll assign that duty to you!" Delaney looked surprised which pleased the Air Marshal. "I know you've wanted to try your hand at this sort of intelligence craft, so here's your chance." The Marshal now held a piece of paper up and gave it to Delaney. "I've already issued orders to have you assigned, temporarily, to Military Intelligence, so do keep me posted, Captain Delaney."

"A promotion, Sir?" It was said with some amazement.

"Yes," he quipped, "you deserve it,."

"Thank you, Sir," and then Delaney turned and looked out the window. "Appears we have some clouds tonight," and pointed, "but look at those stars."

"Why yes," the Marshall replied as he motioned with his right hand. "There's the hunter, Orion."

"With faithful Cirrus just behind," Delaney countered. "That's a good sign."

"Yes, a very good sign indeed for they make a good pair," and the Marshall smiled ever so slightly as he added, "just like we do, lad."

"Indeed," he answered, but he could see that the Marshall looked tired. "Well, I'll say good night, your Lordship."

"Good night" he murmured. After Delaney left, the Air Marshall stared out his window again and noticed that a large cloud seemed to be headed towards the Orion cluster now while a general mist from the Thames was rising. "Well," he muttered, "seems a fog is coming in," then turned and headed for his dressing area to ready himself for bed.

While he did so, the cloud that was headed for the Orion cluster grew ever larger. Eventually, it combined with the massive river's mist and soon they both enveloped most of London's cityscape.

After he returned to his window seat, dressed in pajamas and robe, he was amazed at how thick the fog had become. "Remarkable," he muttered as he picked up the Lossberg file. Although the Air Marshall's heart medicine was nearby, along with a glass of water, he disregarded these just as he ignored how the bedroom windows had begun to streak with moisture. "Strange," he grumbled as he put the file down and picked up the 'Top Secret' file again. "This can't be the same man Stoker saw in France." It was at that moment that a sharp pain in the Air Marshall's chest distracted him. "Must be something I ate," he moaned, and tried to belch to relieve the discomfort. When that didn't help, he suddenly realized what was really going on. He moaned pitifully, dropped the file, and fell to the floor.

TEN

While Delaney was returning to his quarters, an unsettling sensation came over him. "Odd," he muttered as he paused on the staircase's upper landing, then turned and stared up towards the Marshall's suite. While Delaney hesitated an inner apprehension nagged at him and as he fought to control his gut feeling, he remembered what the Surgeon had said once in a counseling session, "Remember," McDougall advised, "these attacks will be like a coaster- you've seen too much for your brain to forget, so what you have to do is to let go, ride them out." Since the Surgeon had been in France, a field doctor in the British Expeditionary Force who had been at the Somme, when he spoke, it was from experience, and veterans, like Delaney, appreciated that. "Now," the Surgeon concluded calmly, "I'll give you a prayer to use, 'God, grant me the serenity to accept the things I cannot change, the courage to change the things I can, and the wisdom to know the difference.' It's an old wisdom," the Surgeon added, "but very adaptable for us so don't be impatient with yourself, and use the prayer when you need it," Tonight, Delaney recited the prayer quickly as he stood there on the stairs, but for some urgent feeling he had, the recitation didn't help. "No," he muttered decisively, "this isn't the same."

Without thinking, the old survival instinct took over and propelled him up one step, then two steps, then up the remaining treads. As he ran down the corridor, he was at the Marshall's door within a few strides. And saw what appeared to be smoke, as it swirled under the door. "Fire," he sputtered as he grabbed the door's handle, but it wasn't hot so he opened the door. Immediately he was greeted by a wave of dense mist. "Your Lordship," Delaney yelled as he went deeper into the mist. The air was heavy, but not uncomfortable to breathe, so he called out again, "Your Lordship?"

"No," a voice from the mist answered.

Delaney stopped. As two red eyes from deep within the mist stared at him, about them there seemed to be a wisp of golden hair that outlined a face.

"I was too late," the figure continued as one of its hands emerged from the mist gestured towards the corpse on the floor. "Some things even I must accept," the emerging figure continued, its eyes never leaving Delaney as the thing moved, ever slightly forward. "Your Major Stoker was a worthy opponent," it continued, "as was Brother Ivan too." The vampire's tone was hypnotic as it asked, "Will you be too, I wonder?"

Delaney felt frozen in place, like he couldn't maneuver, his legs and arms were rigid, and he couldn't take his eyes away from those of the vampire.

As it crept closer, the creature continued speaking, calmly. "Well, Lieutenant, I came here tonight with one purpose in mind, and that was denied me, yet, by luck, look at what I found." The beast held a file in its hand. "I see your operatives have gathered some important insights on me as von Lossberg," and the beast smiled engagingly. "What puzzles me, though," and it gestured with its other hand towards a second file it held, marked 'Top Secret,' "is that I hadn't planned on Major Stoker's accounts, some of which he told to you, would survive the war." The creature was even closer now. "So," the vampire said, its tone quite suggestive, "did Stoker tell you of Brother Ivan's journal and our adventures in the Balkans before the Great War broke out?"

"Yes," Delaney uttered without thinking.

"A remarkable observer, Brother Ivan, was, as was Major Stoker," the vampire remarked coldly. "Well, Lieutenant Delaney, it is time." The beast stood poised to strike. "You must choose whom to serve then."

In his heart, he knew he had no chance against this evil creature. He was powerless to run, to fight, to do much of anything so he let go, trusted in God, and said, "Thy will be done."

Instantly, the vampire snorted in disgust and lunged, but it didn't kill as it drank. After Delaney fainted, the vampire searched the Lieutenant and found nothing. Finally, it rose and looked down and said, with a smirk on its face, "Someday, you'll lead me to Ivan's journal," and formed into a large bat. As it flew out the window, it shrieked, "Till then, live."

After a few minutes, Delaney began to stir, and when he became conscious, it was amazing to him how quiet the room was. Eventually, he moved his hand to his head and then down to the side of his neck where he felt a slight dampness while a fierce headache began. He fought to ignore the pain and rolled over, then, with both hands, began to slowly feel his body. He noticed that his pockets were pulled out., I've been searched, he thought and after a few more seconds, he tried to get up, once, then twice, and finally staggered to his feet. The Air Marshall's body was nearby, laying face down. Delaney turned the corpse over. The body's face looked serene, with no marks, and no blood anywhere so he looked for a pulse and felt none. After that, Delaney straightened himself up and observed that the window was slightly ajar, the curtains softly swaying. The fog had receded back towards the river and as he took stock of all of this, he finally went over to the nightstand, picked up the phone, and dialed the Surgeon's extension.

"Yes?" a sleepy voice answered after a few rings, "what is it?"

"Sir, Lieutenant Delaney here. I'm in his Lordship's chambers and I'm afraid he's suffered a fateful heart episode."

"What?" the voice sounded startled. "What's that you said?"

"I'm in his Lordship's bedroom, Sir, and I'm afraid the Marshall is gone."

"God," the voice exclaimed, "I'll be right up."

"Should I ring Major Dudley, Sir?"

"Yes," the Flight Surgeon replied hurriedly, "and call the Duty Officer too."

"Very good, Sir,' and Delaney hung up and rang up Major Dudley and after that the Duty Officer. Following these calls, Delaney stood there and tried to touch nothing, but did notice the files the Air Marshall had been reading were gone. "Bloody hell," Delaney muttered as he heard a series of loud and hurried footsteps out in the hallway. Within seconds, Surgeon McDougall came through the door and headed straight for the corpse, thereafter, two more sets of footsteps pounded outside. In a few moments, in rushed Major Dudley and the Duty Officer who went right past the Lieutenant, headed for the Doctor who was still kneeling by the cadaver.

"Is he gone?" Dudley asked, his voice showing signs of strain.

"Yes," McDougall replied as he shook his head, then looked up, "I'm afraid so."

"Stroke?" It was the Duty Officer speaking.

"Appears to be, Captain," then MacDougall stood up. "Quick and easy."

"Not a bad way to go," the Duty Officer countered.

"No, gentleman, it is indeed not," the Surgeon answered. He looked over at Delaney and said, "Lieutenant."

"Sir," he replied.

"Call the military hospital at St. James and have an unmarked ambulance come over. Tell them to be as quiet as they can. No siren, no need to rush."

"Very good, Sir."

"Tell them to use the back entry too," MacDougall added just before Delaney left, then MacDougall turned towards the other two officers. "Gentleman," and he motioned with his arms, "we need to talk." After the others came closer, he continued "We'll have to inform Downing Street, immediately," he said firmly, "and you Major Dudley, must make the call."

"Right, I'm on it."

"Good," the Surgeon said nervously, "but first, we must search around to see if those files the Marshall was looking at are still here."

"Oh, God," Dudley declared, his voice showing his alarm, "are they gone?"

"Indeed," the Surgeon responded gravely, "indeed, it would appear so."

In the meanwhile, Delaney had gone down to Major Dudley's office and called St. James, then went out along the corridor to the rear entrance. As he stood in the small foyer, looking out a glass side panel by the door, he could see the driveway. "What was that thing looking for?" he sputtered just as Big Ben's chimes sounded the quarter hour. Since the pain in his head had become piercing again, he opened the door and went onto the back porch. Immediately, he took out a cigarette, lit it, hoping the nicotine would help ease his suffering. Why didn't it kill me? he thought, then took another puff. While he watched the smoke ring swirl about, the answer came to him. "Ivan's journal," the two words came blurting out just as he heard a vehicle's approach from down the street. Taking one last puff, Delaney flipped the cigarette off. "Well, ya evil bastard," Delaney exclaimed as he looked towards the river, "you didn't get it from me, damn you!"

In the meanwhile, the front headlights of a vehicle appeared down the street. Within a few moments, the ambulance was near enough to the mansion for Delaney to raise his arms. The driver saw this signal and then swung into the driveway, stopped, shifted into reverse, and maneuvered the unmarked ambulance into position. After that, Delaney went down the steps to greet the driver and the other attendant.

"Where's the body, Sir?" the Corporal asked respectfully as he saluted.

"Upstairs," Delaney answered as he pointed to a window on the second floor.

"Who is it, Sir?" asked the other soldier.

"The Air Marshall."

"God," the driver gasped.

As the two medical attendants moved to open the rear doors of the van, the second soldier blurted out, "There'll be the Devil to pay on this."

"Quiet, there," Delaney countered forcefully, trying to control his emotions, as the soldiers removed the stretcher, "let's get this done, so follow me."

Once they had the body in the ambulance and were on their way back to St. James, it was the driver who spoke first. "A bad thing this," and jerked his head back towards the rear of the van, "bad."

"Yes, Mate," the other soldier responded, his tone grim as he continued, "no good will come of this, that's for sure."

"Aye," the former replied as he shifted gears on the truck's steering wheel, "that's for bloody sure."

Meanwhile while Delaney watched the ambulance drive off, he stayed in control of his emotions, but once the van turned the corner and had disappeared, he sat down on the steps and placing his head between his hands, he began to sob, uncontrollably.

Inside the house, Major Dudley was completing his call to the Prime Minister. "Yes," he asked, "and you say both files are missing after your search?"

"Yes," Major Dudley answered, his tone showing his frustration, "both are gone, Prime Minister."

"Well," he replied, "keep me informed, Major, as you can." The Prime Minister hung up the phone, shook his head, and muttered, "Good God, almighty." After a few lingering moments, he sat down in his bedroom chair and blurted out, "God help us all."

Meanwhile, up in the clouds, like a professional ballroom dancer, the vampire twisted and turned in a waltz of evil, happily gliding across the sky. It was well satisfied at its performance at the Air Marshal's house, happy that Satan's plan was still progressing onwards, happy that the new millennium was becoming more and more a reality, happily purring, "Soon, soon."

ELEVEN

The black Mercedes was roaring down the highway, its small red and brown fender flags fluttering as the driver, a young member of the Staff Guard, kept his eyes securely on the road that helped him ignore the passionate sounds emanating from the rear of the sedan. He had seen much since entering the Storm Troops or SA, but there were times of late when he wondered if the sexcapades of some of its senior members were becoming decadent. He wasn't a naive person, yet tonight, even though the curtains were drawn, the sounds from the back seat were testing his limits. He hoped that tonight's duty would be over soon, but traffic in the city had been heavy and so the car had been delayed. "Damn," he sputtered, as he looked at his watch in the dim light of the dashboard's display, "it's a quarter to," and so urged the car's massive engine forward.

"Make sure you drive carefully," the blond SA Staff Major had said arrogantly to the driver when tonight's couple first approached the car, the lovely figure of a woman in a full length black hooded cape on the Major's arm. "Remember," he snapped to the driver who held the rear door open, "we must be there by nine," then skillfully assisted his date into the seat. That had been 30 minutes ago and the driver was nervous now that he wouldn't be at the villa by 9 P.M. He had been assigned to the

Staff Guard for over a year and had been proud to join the Guards, but ever since being assigned to these particular escort duties, he had begun to doubt the character of some senior Brown Shirt authorities.

Just then, he saw an off lane coming up, marked by a clump of Rowan trees. When he saw the lane marker, he eased off the highway, turned left, and headed down a spruce lined driveway. From past trips, he knew the gatehouse would be about a quarter of a kilometer from the turn off. While he gently approached the white gatekeeper's cottage, several armed SA Staff Guards in their brown overcoats and white helmets, immediately recognized the car and raised the road barrier. As he motored up the graveled driveway towards the stately Italianate mansion formerly owned by a Jewish merchant, who after some ugly pressure, had given it to the SA, the villa seemed to shimmer with lights. He slowed the car to a stop in front of the main entrance and could see that many couples were on the side terraces. The sounds of their laughter mingled with the music from inside, for there was a grand party in sway tonight.

As if on cue, two SA Staff waiters in white jackets and brown pants came down the steps. Each was a blond, groomed impeccably, and while the driver gripped the steering wheel, watching in the side mirror, the rear door was opened. After several long and awkward moments, the SA Major emerged and began to straighten his uniform, then smoothed his ruffled hair. As he placed his cap rakishly on his head, he turned back to the car, extended his hand, and crooned, "May I."

As the driver watched, a long white gloved hand extended, grasped the SA Major's fingers, and in one powerful swoop, he pulled and out came the tart whose black satin gown was cut up to the thigh. As the Major held her, her long platinum blond hair cascaded down the back of the dress while she discreetly held a white fan in her left hand which obscured her features. In an instant though, as he leaned in for a kiss, she dropped the fan into a single fold that revealed her face. "Section Leader Junker?" the driver blurted out, but before he could utter another word, the feminine figure turned back towards the Major and the mirror's angle was lost.

It was a tap on the driver's window that startled him. "Move along," a waiter snarled dismissively, then added, "Put it out back," and signaled to the left, "over there. You'll be called when they're ready to leave."

The waiter's mocking tone angered the trooper, but he made no response as he shifted the car back into gear and drove round the circle towards the car park. A haze was forming as he pulled into the rear lot where five more SA staff cars were already parked and after he found a vacant space, parked, and got out. He couldn't see any other drivers since the mist now obscured most of the area, so he reached for a cigarette, found one in his tunic's pocket, and lit up. He was on his second drag when a voice, quite near, spoke.

"Going to be a long night." It was said nonchalantly as if the speaker was ready to say more, but didn't want to just yet.

The driver turned, and to his amazement saw an SS Major there. The driver snapped to attention and as he did dropped his cigarette, the burning parchment quickly lost in the enveloping fog.

"Is this to your liking?" the Major asked as he lazily extended his arm and pointed towards the villa.

"I obey orders, Herr Major," the driver answered reflexively.

"That is not what I asked you," the Major sneered. "Do those Sodomites please you, Private?"

"No," the driver answered without hesitation. As he stared into the SS Major's eyes, the Private felt compelled to repeat, "no, Herr Major."

"Why is that?"

"It is decadent," the driver muttered as the SS Major moved closer.

"Decadence has its place," the officer responded, suggesting he expected the trooper to say more.

"No," the driver continued, surprised at his ability to say what he really thought, "but decadence is not good if we serve the true cause."

"Do you serve Rohm or Hitler?" the Major asked pointedly.

"De Fuhrer," the trooper snapped.

"Well," the vampire crooned as it drew back its head. It looked long and hard at the trooper and said, finally, "Good."

The driver stood transfixed, but his heart was racing.

"Be in my office at 8 P.M," the SS Major continued as he drew a card from his tunic and thrust it towards the trooper. "There is no turning back now for you have chosen, little brother. Remember all you see here," and motioned towards the villa. "Report names to me." The vampire titled its head like a bird of prey. "Understand?"

"Yes," the terrified driver replied.

While the beast drew back even further, the fog swirled about in denser clouds, and within seconds, the black clad SS officer was gone.

"Damn," the driver uttered as the mist began to clear, and when he finally was able read the Major's calling card, the driver recognized the officer's name. "What a hell of a night," the trooper mumbled as he put the card away. After that, he decided to get back into the car and make himself as comfortable as possible, while the party in the villa raged on with unabated fervor.

While this was going on, the vampire went back to the city feeling good that another recruit had been enlisted in Satan's army. The beast was well pleased too with the kill made at the soiree earlier that had satisfied its hunger, so there was no more need to feed tonight. The creature was making directly to the Fuhrer's Berlin headquarters and once inside, it reformed into the SS Major. After arriving at Hitler's office, the Major was immediately ushered in. Hitler waited till the door was closed, then rose from his desk and dropped to one knee as the beast extended its hand. "Rise, little brother," the vampire said after Hitler kissed the beast's ring, "for there is much to be done in the next few weeks." Hitler said nothing as he stood up. "This feuding between the Brown Shirts, the SS, and the Army drains us," Satan's agent continued, "so we must sacrifice one to control the other now. Blood must be shed to resolve this matter."

"Whose Lord?" Hitler asked expectantly

"Rohm must go," the vampire snarled, "for his brown shirted army is an undisciplined mob."

"It will be hard to lose an old friend," Hitler replied.

"Yes, I know," the vampire replied, "it will be hard to lose Rohm, he has been there from the beginning, but we must do this thing," the creature replied as it put a hand on Hitler's shoulder. "We must show the SS and the Army just how ruthless you can be, Wolf, besides the Rohm's SA has become too degenerate. Have you not heard the stories about their sexcapades?"

"Yes," Hitler answered, his voice almost a whisper.

"A house divided," and the beast laughed, for it knew of Hitler's sexual prudishness. "Pleasure has its uses," the creature continued, "but no man can serve both pleasure and Satan. Rohm's men have chosen pleasure and decadence, and now we shall use their destruction to our advantage against the Army."

Hitler waited impatiently, but knew enough not to interrupt.

The beast was pacing as it went on speaking. "By this bloody act against the SA, we shall lose them, but from its death, we shall control the Army, for they will see our purge of Rohm's men as eliminating a strong opponent to their precious and growing military's status," the vampire thundered. "The Army's pride will be their downfall." The words were gushing from the beast now. "They do not fear the SS yet," and the creatures stopped, paused, "but they will, eventually, for we shall build the SS up from this action against Rohm. Himmler's Storm troopers will be our gambit to control the Army."

"Lord," Hitler replied, "Himmler is no Rohm."

"True, but that SS bookkeeper can kill just as ruthlessly. After the Brown Shirts are destroyed, we shall give him some military weapons and allow his men to become your elite warriors, your Life Guards."

"The generals will not stand for the creation of the SS as a military branch," Hitler countered confidently. "They will object, and they will howl at me to restrain the SS."

"Yes," the beast said, the word deliberately sneered through its teeth, "so we'll let the generals think that if they join with us now as you purge the SA to ensure your power as the Fuhrer, Himmler won't become your spear point. The destruction of the Brown Shirts will let those old Prussians think we might offer the SS up someday too as another sacrifice, just like we did to Rohm," and the vampire clapped it hands. "Rohm's destruction by the SS will be the blood act that binds the Generals, heart and soul, to us. Those old Prussians fear the SA as a rival military force. You can make a deal with the generals now before you destroy Rohm, and once they see his destruction, they'll know the bargain you made with them was real."

"But how can we agree to such a deal with the Army?" Hitler asked hesitantly.

"What we agree to," the vampire countered, "and what we really do, are two different things. Call it the big lie if you want," and the beast smiled wickedly at its disciple, "so we'll need to play this close to the chest, little brother. We have to snare the Army carefully, but once we get them to think they might own you through your bargain with them, that they, not the SS, shall be the foundation of your power in the future. As a result of the deal you'll make with the Army, we shall have those aristocratic noblemen, so get them to agree to support you by destroying your old friend, Rohm."

"Yes, Lord, I shall summon the General Staff tomorrow and make the bargain."

"Good and then, before those old Prussians know it, we shall have each soldier in the Army, swear by personal oath, their allegiance directly to you, the Fuhrer."

"The soldiers shall pledge themselves to me, Lord, and not the nation?"

"Yes," the vampire said triumphantly. "We shall demand it through the Reichstag's passage of a new law. Each regiment, each battalion, each company will swear fidelity to you, upon their sacred regimental flags. All will raise their hands in loyalty, all will become sworn to you, and it will be a glorious ceremony, Wolf, a glorious chapter in the reign of the Third Reich."

Hitler smiled.

"Here," the beast continued as it handed Hitler a list it drew from its uniform, "are the names that must be purged."

Hitler took the list and read it quickly.

"There will be more," the beast said calmly, "after tonight."

"Yes, Lord."

"Remember," the beast commanded, "no one is to be spared once his name appears there," and it pointed to the index in Hitler's hands. "No mercy and no pity."

"I will be ruthless Lord," Hitler answered as he looked up from the list. "Himmler's SS men have been trained to kill since the Enabling Act, so I will instruct that they should be ruthless too."

"Good," the creature said. "When do you next meet with Rohm?"

"Tomorrow, Lord."

"Be pleasant," the vampire said with a twinkle in its eyes. "Hold Rohm close, just like a friend." The beast's tone sounded amusing as it continued. "It is a trick I've taught some of my Italian friends, long, long ago."

"Yes," Hitler replied knowingly of the old Machiavellian adage.

"Call in Himmler tonight and set his wolves upon the SA. Do this cleansing within a fortnight," and the creature pointed at his disciple. "There will be another series of sexual sorties soon and we'll use the pleasures of the flesh to trap Rohm and his top followers. Be cruel" and it glared at Hitler, "be heartless." Suddenly, the vampire turned its back on Hitler and as it strode away, said, "I shall be watching."

Once Hitler was sure the beast had left, the Fuhrer looked at the list again, and there, at the top in red ink was Ernst Rohm's name. "Well, old comrade," Hitler muttered, "we know a general has to order the thing he loves the most to battle and to possible death," then Hitler sighed. After a few seconds, he pressed the button on his intercom and said, "Send for Himmler."

"Yes, Mein Fuhrer," came the reply.

After a few minutes, Himmler was let in and as he came across the floor with his aide, Colonel Kurt Sturmer, both men had a certain swagger to their stride. Himmler's was based upon his loftiness as SS Reichleader; Sturmer's was based upon his Aryan features and attitudes. When in front of the Fuhrer, they stopped and raised their arms and spoke, "Hail Hitler."

Hitler raised his arm slightly in response, saying, "Gentlemen," and swept his arm downwards, "be seated," and looked directly at Himmler who seemed lost in his uniform. Hitler knew of the ruthlessness this fragile man could summon up, of the passion he could muster to be merciless and was well with it, so far. "Look at this," the Fuhrer said as he passed the index of names across the desktop. After that, Hitler purposely turned his gaze to Sturmer and thought, now here is the faithful dog that will do anything to serve its master, then smiled charmingly.

As if he was wagging his tail to his master, Sturmer smiled back.

"I have decided," Hitler cooed while Himmler continued to read the list, "that this squabbling has to end," and suddenly slammed the desk with the palm of his hand. "The SA has grown soft and victory has made them weak," Hitler shrieked, pleased to see his display of controlled anger was working. "The SA must be purged," and while Hitler watched, Sturmer's chest rose in anticipation and his head twitched slightly while his lips opened just barely. Like a great cat, his tongue stuck out just a fraction too as he waited in anticipation.

"All," Himmler replied as he calmly scanned the list.

"All," Hitler snapped back.

"When?" the Reichleader asked.

"In two weeks," the Fuhrer responded as he folded his hands together in satisfaction. "I've been informed that there will be other gatherings then, so that's the time to strike," and Hitler smiled sweetly. "They won't be expecting it."

Himmler passed the list to Sturmer. When he saw the first name, he blushed, then muttered, "Rohm, too."

"Even old comrades, Colonel," Hitler replied sternly. "Hard decisions need to be made, gentlemen, and we need strong men to make our rule secure. Ruthless men, men of vision for we must leave decadence behind in order to build our new order and consequently, I have chosen you, the SS, to be my champions." Hitler was looking at Himmler, playing upon the Reichleader's hopes, since he had aspirations of making the SS the model of the new Aryan order. "I'll leave the details of this assignment up to you, Reichleader," the Fuhrer said, pointing his finger, "but the least I know from this point on, the better."

"Yes," Himmler answered, a slight smile upon his lips. "I understand you meet with Chief of Staff Rohm tomorrow, my Fuhrer."

"Yes, we have a scheduled luncheon together," and Hitler cracked his own mischievous smile, but his mirth faded instantly. "We shall be discussing the SA's future." Suddenly and on purpose, Hitler pounded the table again, "So Reichleader, attend to Rohm in what we shall call The Night of the Long Knives."

"So it is ordered, my Fuhrer," Himmler quipped, "so shall it be done."

Hitler nodded approvingly.

"Good night, my Fuhrer." Himmler said politely as he rose. Instantly, Sturmer stood up too.

"Yes," Hitler replied nonchalantly as he yawned, showing his usual mock fatigue at the end of a meeting.

As the two SS officers walked silently down the corridor, past the guards, and out to into a waiting car, it was Sturmer who spoke first. "We have won." His voice was triumphant. "The SA will be eliminated."

"Yes, Sturmer," Himmler replied cautiously, "it would seem we have been authorized to destroy one enemy but other enemies exist."

"You seem worried Reichleader?"

"No, Sturmer, just reflective. We are too weak at present to take on the Army since Rohm and his Brown Shirts were our shield against those old Prussians generals. The Fuhrer gives us more power now and after this purge, we shall grow stronger for is that not what the Fuhrer intends from this blood letting?"

"Yes," the Colonel answered immediately, "and our ranks will swell as we become the Fuhrer's Life Guards."

"Yes," Himmler said slowly then he looked directly at Sturmer, "for we are bound, heart and soul, to de Fuhrer. We shall become the swords around his throne, just as in the old days of the Aryan warriors."

"Indeed," Sturmer replied, a wide smile on his face, "indeed we shall."

Himmler nodded and when he continued, his voice took on a mystic tone. "We are forged into a mighty weapon of steel ever since the creation of Dachau, Sturmer, and we shall strike hard upon the Fuhrer's enemies."

Sturmer nodded.

"This strike against the SA will the night of the long knives," Himmler continued, but then fell quiet, as if this outburst was too much for his frail body. After a while, he spoke again, "But I am reminded of an old Greek saying, 'Who kills his own, scorns both God and man.'"

"Do you fear the Fuhrer then, Herr Riechleader?" Sturmer asked.

"Yes," Himmler answered, "and so should you," but Sturmer made no reply. Within a few minutes, the SS staff car was slowing as it approached Himmler's compound, and so he asked, "How many men will you need?"

"A battalion will be enough," Sturmer replied methodically, "as long as they are equipped as mobile units and linked by radio."

He's a good killer, Himmler thought, but didn't say so, instead said, "Strike hard," then the Reichleader pounded the vehicle's armrest. "Let none escape, so snare them all, these decadent men, these seekers of flesh, these Sodomites and boozers for they corrupt us from within and weaken our good Aryan blood."

"It will be done, Herr Reichleader."

"Make sure to document it too, Colonel," Himmler continued, "for we want to show the Fuhrer some good pictures." Himmler chuckled at this, then added, "since you know how the Fuhrer likes his movies."

"We shall have cameras on hand, Herr Reichleader."

"Good," he replied as the car came to a stop. "I shall leave you to it then, Colonel," and Himmler gave the list, the index of names, to his right hand man. "Give me an initial report by tomorrow evening."

"Yes, I will Reichleader." While an SS guard opened the door, Sturmer exited quickly, headed for his aide, Captain Holst, who was standing on the building's steps.

"Is it what we hoped for, Colonel?" Captain Holst asked excitedly as the Reichleader's car sped off.

"And more, Holst, and more," Sturmer replied as he held up the file, "but let's get inside." After that they went immediately to the Colonel's office where Sturmer asked, "Drink, Captain?"

"Yes, thank you, Sir."

After the Colonel opened his desk drawer, he took out two tumblers, then a bottle of schnapps. When the glasses were a quarter full, Sturmer gave one to Holst, took the other, raised it, and said, "Proust." After they drained each tumbler, Sturmer continued, "We have some house cleaning to do Holst, for we have been authorized to bring fire and sword to those SA wimps. Fire and sword, Captain, fire and sword."

"When, Herr Colonel?"

"Two weeks," Sturmer replied as he poured another drink for them a grand smile on his face, "so we'll work out the plan tonight."

Holst was waiting expectantly now.

"We present the details to Himmler tomorrow evening," Sturmer said as he raised his glass, and took a sip, then finished his sentence, "so we'll be here for a while."

"May I phone my wife, Colonel?" the Captain asked for he had been recently married to a good Aryan female. Sturmer had been there, as an honored guest, and so had lent approval to the marriage, as a part of the new order of things in Germany.

"Yes, but be quick," and Sturmer winked.

Captain Holst put his glass down, saluted, and left.

"He's as happy as a pup," Sturmer muttered as he sat down and began to sketch out a plan for the SA's destruction. About five minutes later, the Captain returned and took his place by his Colonel's side. "Here's the basic plan," Sturmer said as he shoved a piece of paper across the desk. "What do you think?"

Holst studied it, and after a few moments said, "Yes, this will work," then saw a look of concern on Sturmer's face so asked, somewhat nervously, "Is there a problem?"

"Killing doesn't bother me, Holst, no killing is only a means to an end, a useful tool. Business really," and the Colonel laughed at his jest. "No Holst, what bothers me on this job is that we are killing some of our own. Rohm was with the Fuhrer from the beginning. He was the creator of the Hall Guards." There was fire in Sturmer tone as he continued, "Rohm's heart," and Sturmer pounded his heaving chest dramatically, "was with the Fuhrer then."

"But Colonel," Holst countered before Sturmer could go on, "are we not bound to the Fuhrer too?" Holst's voice conveyed an equal passion to Sturmer's as the Captain continued, "Hasn't Rohm contradicted the Fuhrer before. Wasn't that why Rohm was exiled to Bolivia once by the Party?"

Sturmer made no reprimand for Holst's interruption, Sturmer just waited for he wanted to see what else his Aide had to say. Sturmer was testing his Aide to see if Holst was truly an SS man in light of the order to destroy the Brown Shirts.

"We, the SS, are the elite order, Colonel," Holst exclaimed as he went on, full of himself, of what he was. "The old males, like Rohm, grow weak. They allow too much and they can no longer rule the pride." Holst's eyes were bright with passion as he continued. "It is we who must rise, like the young lions. Is this not the destiny for which the Fuhrer is preparing us? Do we not owe all, everything, to the Fuhrer? Is he not our Lord, our Creator, our Master?"

"What of God?" Sturmer countered.

"There is no God," Holst answered, his face radiant, glowing as he proclaimed, "only the Fuhrer, my Colonel."

"Damn," Sturmer declared as he slapped his desk's top, "I like you, Holst."

"Sir," he answered with the pride of a true believer.

"The Fuhrer is our Father, Son, and Holy Ghost!" Sturmer exclaimed triumphantly, "so I am glad you understand fully then," and the Colonel clapped his hands. "The Night of the Long Knives, that's what we'll call the destruction of the Brown Shirts, and how we in the SS shall enjoy it, Holst, how very, very much, indeed!"

TWELVE

Following the Great Depression, Miller's job at the restaurant was gone, but since he had been frequenting a small private airfield outside the city for years, he had made friends with the chief mechanic there, an older Army veteran, named Rinehart Finst. One day, Finst, who desperately needed a good helper, said to the now unemployed Miller, "I can't pay you, but I can give you food and board and teach you to fly if you stay and help me."

"I'll take it," Miller said, so the two struck a deal whereby Miller moved into a small room in the hanger and began his apprenticeship. Since flying clubs in Germany were very popular, there was a steady flow of men and planes at the airfield, especially after the 1932 election that saw Hitler and his party placed into power. Miller's life revolved around the airport, until one day, in 1935, an eagle eyed Luftwaffe Major of the reconstituted German air force visited the small airdrome to meet with Finst.

"He is a born pilot, Herr Major, and he has agility," Finst said with confidence as they met in the airfield's small office, "and I have given Miller knowledge of all types of aircraft these past few years."

"Will he make a good candidate?" the Major asked.

"He will be a good Luftwaffe candidate, I think," Finst replied assuredly.

"I trust your judgment, Rinehart," the Major responded as he looked over Miller's file, closed it, and said, "So, this Miller is a veteran too," and looked at Finst carefully, "and what of Miller's family?"

"He is not a Jew, Herr Major," Finst snapped, "just a Bavarian."

"Ya," the Major replied with a chuckle over the old jab about Bavarians that Finst, a fellow Prussian, had made. "Well," the Major continued as he drew in a breath, "we even took them in the old Squadron in the last war." The Major's aristocratic tone continued on as he spoke. "Miller's a bit old for fighters," the Major concluded with an air of finality, "maybe a bomber pilot, I think."

"Yes, Herr Major," Finst, the former sergeant in the old Imperial Air Force, replied since he knew how to keep his place when a superior had made a decision.

"Well now, bring Miller to me." the Major commanded.

"Very good, Sir." Finst left and went into the hanger. "Ludwig, over here," Finst called out to Miller who was working on a plane. "Come, come quickly."

"What is it, Rinehart?" Miller asked expectantly as he came near.

"Your chance has arrived," and Rinehart slapped Miller on the shoulder. "Are you ready?"

He nodded for he had seen the Major and Finst entering the office together.

"Good," he continued. "Now remember what I told you," and Finst turned, "so come with me." Once inside, he came up to the desk and snapped to attention. "Herr Major, his is my able apprentice, Ludwig Miller."

Eyeing Miller carefully, the Prussian officer's tone was judicial as he began, "Herr Finst is an old comrade from the war and I value his opinion, so do not disappoint either of us," the Major said as he inspected Miller who stood at attention. "We need good men, Miller, especially candidates for flyers as we expand the air force, but you are too old for fighters." Miller felt his heart skip a beat, but before his disappointment could take hold, the Major continued, "A good steady hand for bombers will do the Reich nicely, so Miller, so are you prepared to train hard and obey faithfully?"

"Yes, Herr Major," Miller replied as he looked straight ahead, seeing his future in the Luftwaffe looming ahead.

"Well," the Major grunted, "we'll see, so now Recruit Miller, collect your belongings and report to my driver, dismissed."

The mechanic clicked his heels, but didn't give a Nazi salute, then left.

After Miller had gone, Finst spoke. "A good start, Sir?"

"Yes," he said with a thin smile on his lips, for he too had noticed Miller's lack of the Nazi salute. "You have done well, old comrade."

"Thank you, Sir," Finst answered as his chest swelled with pride.

"When the new war comes, Rinehart," the Major began slowly, "we will need good old soldiers like you, too," then paused, "so stay well." Immediately, Finst saluted, but not in the new Nazi salute, but in the old Army way. The Major stood up and returned the salute in the old way too. "Remember, my friend," the Major whispered, "we must be careful," and then the Major arched his eye brow, "so learn the new salute, ya?"

Rinehart nodded. "Indeed," the Major continued as he took up his gloves and slapped them in his left hand. "Well, old comrade, I must be going," then, with Miller's file in hand, headed for the door without another word.

"Well, Miller," Finst muttered after the Major had gone, "your future is ahead of you now," then Finst went out into the hanger. "Let's see," he sputtered as he spotted the biplane Miller had been working on, "Ah, Number Three," and headed off well satisfied that a new pilot recruit had been obtained for the rebuilding German Air Force, the new Luffwaffe of the Third Reich.

In the meanwhile, Miller had gotten his few possessions together in his duffel bag and reported to the Major's car where the driver told the mechanic to get in the front passenger seat. After the Major had arrived and was shown in, the driver hopped into the car, started the engine, and roared off. Miller observed that the window was up between the rear passenger's seat and the front, but the driver had his own window down a bit. It was then that Miller noticed the smell, and remembered he still had his working clothes on. "Sorry about that," he muttered to the driver.

"No need," he replied as he kept his eyes on the road. "I'm used to it."

"Well, I passed this test" the former mechanic said, his tone hopeful.

"Yes," the driver curtly countered, "and there will be more."

"Oh," Miller replied and fell silent for he knew enough, having been in the Army, when to shut up. After a few minutes though, he saw that they were headed north, away from the city.

After about a half hour of silence, the driver spoke again, "We'll be there soon, so remember, if you want to make it here, obey, ask no questions. Just do whatever they say, instantly, and quickly."

"Thanks."

"Right," the driver responded then concentrated on his driving.

Although Miller was glad for the man's advice, he felt compelled to feel for his Saint Christopher's medal, but he did it carefully, as if he was scratching his chest. The gesture helped to calm him and made the rest of the ride bearable.

Eventually, the vehicle came to a military checkpoint, but didn't slow as the gate's yellow and blue barrier went up. While a squad of Luftwaffe soldiers stood at attention, the automobile continued on inside the aerodome, made a hard turn, then approached a row of barracks and slowed. By then, a sergeant had come out of the middle barracks and stood at attention on the plank sidewalk. After the vehicle stopped, the Major had already rolled down his window and called out, "A new pigeon, Sergeant!"

"Yes, Herr Major," the Sergeant barked back, a wicked smile on his face.

"See if you can make an eagle out of him," the Major remarked flippantly and with that handed Miller's file over.

"Move," the driver said to Miller who grabbed his bag and moved out quickly.

While the car roared off, creating a film of dust, the bull-faced sergeant just stared at Miller. "Christ, what piece of shit do we have here," the sergeant roared as he motioned towards a spot on the sidewalk. "Move!" After Miller did, the Sergeant looked over Miller's file after which he glanced up. "So, Miller, you're a veteran, are ya," and moved closer and got into Miller's face. "What outfit?"

"2nd Bavarian Infantry Regiment, Sergeant," Miller shouted.

"Well," the sergeant cracked back, "that's something, Recruit Miller, but look at your clothes! Didn't have time to change properly, did you?"

Miller knew not to respond to such a question.

"Well, scum," the sergeant yelled, satisfied at Miller's actions so far, "let's get you cleaned up and see if we can make an officer out of you yet." As they began to proceed across the street, headed towards a building marked "Reception," Miller got in step. He remained a pace behind the sergeant though, something he noted pleasurably, but didn't show any visible sign of. Well, he thought, at least I've got something to work with this time.

Thus began Miller's career in the expanding Luftwaffe, a chance that promised him a new life to fulfill a dream, but one that also, ultimately, put his soul in jeopardy. For the moment though, Recruit Miller, Officer Candidate Miller, felt comfortable. Little did he realize that the avenues to Hell are paved differently for each man, especially if they remain unaware of what is really going happening..

As Hitler's Germany began to massively rearm, in direct violation of the Treaty of Versailles, Satan's plans for a new millennium of evil were progressing quite nicely.

THIRTEEN

While the procession of big, black, four-door Mercedes convertibles cruised slowly along the flag draped *Via Triumphales* headed for the Olympic Stadium, the huge crowds of twenty to thirty deep that lined the garlanded boulevard were held in check by over forty thousand SS Storm Troopers and policemen. "Quite a parade," United Press Correspondent Frank Cornwall yelled towards Jamie Bloomberg, a fellow correspondent while they stood watching the motorcade's final approach towards the stadium. "Looks like the circus is coming to town."

"There he is," someone shouted excitedly before Bloomberg could reply.

"All hail the conquering hero," he quipped as he pointed towards Hitler's car.

"Yeah," Cornwall snapped back, his tone loaded with sarcasm, "the proconsul is here so let the bread and circuses begin!" While thousands clapped wildly, fortunately for the reporters, few in the throng had heard the two reporters.

It was near 4 P.M., and the line of cars was coming to the parade grounds near the west end of the stadium. After they stopped, the dignitaries exited and the entourage prepared to enter through a tunnel dubbed, "The Marathon Gate."

"Let's get inside," Bloomberg remarked, "this should be quite an entrance."

"Right," Cornwall replied. As they began to trot up the tunnel, they were directed to the International Press area just before the tunnel's entrance was to be sealed off by the security guards.

Hitler, meanwhile, followed closely by the Bulgarian King, the crown princes of Italy, Greece and Sweden, along with Mussolini's sons and members of the International Olympic Committee, advanced into the tunnel. When they were near the stadium's side entrance, thirty black clad SS trumpeters began to blast a fanfare over the electronically amplified speakers. Instantly, the crowd of over one hundred and ten thousand was on their feet, roaring their approval.

"And now entering the main ring," Cornwall boomed in his best public announcer's voice, "ladies and gentlemen, boys and girls, the famous Picklegruber and Krantz Circus is proud to present," and he paused and waved towards Hitler down below, "the one, the only, the Aryan Nation's proudest performer, Adolph Hitler and his band of Nordic supermen!"

Few in the stadium or in the International Press area heard Cornwall's introduction though, but Bloomberg, who stood next to Cornwall, did. "Some day, Frank," Bloomberg muttered as he motioned towards an SS attendant just a few meters away, "they're gonna hear ya," and then Jamie drew his finger across his throat.

"Ah, nuts," Frank sputtered, a wry smile on his face.

At that very moment, the stadium erupted with new waves of cheers. While Hitler continued his promenade to the reviewing stand as the trumpets' fanfare ended, the world famous Conductor, Richard Strauss, signaled the huge orchestra and chorus of three thousand performers to begin playing

"Deutschland uber alles." As the tune's rich melody and harmonies swelled, the arrangement brought tears of joy and pride to many in the audience.

"*The Entrance of the Gladiators* would have been better, if you ask me," Cornwall mumbled as Hitler strode across the platform.

Just then, above the stadium, the airship *Hindenburg* appeared. As it glided there, it trailed a massive banner with the Olympic flag on it. The sight of both of these caused many in the audience to point and shout with joy.

"Quite a show," Bloomberg commented, but Cornwall just shook his head.

When the first song finished, a second one, the "Horst Wessellied" commenced. With that popular Nazi tune playing, the crowd began to sing along. Finally, in a musical crescendo, that song ended and was blended into the new "Olympic Hymn." The whole time these songs were being played, Hitler's party was standing on the main stage in front of their seats. Goring was on Hitler's left, dressed in a sky-blue Luftwaffe Marshall's uniform while Goebbels, the Reich Minister of Propaganda, was on the right and wore an all white business suit. Hitler, by stark contrast, stood between then and was attired in a brown drab uniform that was markedly highlighted by Goring and Goebbels uniforms. These leaders' clothes and positioning of where they stood were all a part of the event's staging and played well before the multitudes.

Following the end of the "Olympic Hymn," but before the dignitaries were seated, a little girl in pigtails and cap, wearing traditional Germanic dress, emerged from the gathering on the stage. She came up to Hitler, bowed, and handed the Fuhrer a small bouquet of wild flowers. He bent over, took the gift, and smiled at her in a fatherly way, grinning pleasantly all the while.

"Right on cue," Cornwall quipped as he elbowed his fellow American.

"Amazing," Bloomberg countered, "Buzzy Berkeley in Hollywood couldn't have done better than this."

"That's show biz, Kiddo," Cornwall countered as he cocked his head and added, "Hitler's smooth."

After the child left, Hitler sat down while the crowd murmured its collective approval with a round of uhs and ahs.

"He's real class," Cornwall sneered quietly, "I'll give the bastard that," but before Bloomberg could answer, the massive bell atop the Glockenturm at the Maifield Stadium tolled. Its deep peeling caught them, and the audience, by surprise. At a thirty-second timed intervals, the bell rang out, then stopped, and rang out again. With each peel, the tone seemed to quell the audience's noise more. Finally, after the bell's third toll echoed, the stadium's lights went dark, and several spotlights flashed on the darkened entrance of the Marathon Gage. With that dramatic effect, the eyes of the audience turned and beheld the leading elements of the parade of athletes moving into view.

First out of the tunnel was the Greek team in the honored Olympic position who were then followed by the Egyptians, since, in German, *Aegypten*, preceded all other nations in attendance. As the other teams marched in, each had its nation's flag at the front carried by an honored standard bearer. When they neared the reviewing stand, the team members gave the new Olympic salute, an arm out to the side with the palm of the hand down.

"Look at that," Bloomberg exclaimed in disgust.

"Christ," Cornwall answered, "it's almost like the Nazi salute."

"Damn," Bloomberg muttered, his voice showing his disdain, "I hope we don't use it when our team passes by."

When the Austrian team greeted Hitler, it was in the Nazi fashion with their arms held forward, hands raised upward. Seeing this Nazi salute, the crowd applauded loudly for they understood the Austrian gesture.

"Won't be long before he gets Austria into the Reich, Kiddo," Cornwall growled as he moved closer toward his friend. Cornwall knew Bloomberg's parents were Jewish, originally from Vienna, and that the sight of the Austrian team's display must have hurt.

"Too bad for the Austrians," Bloomberg muttered as he turned and looked towards an SS attendant who had come closer. It was apparent the SS trooper wished to hear more of what the Americans were saying. "We've got company," Bloomberg whispered to Cornwall.

He nodded sweetly at the SS man and then pointed back out towards the track where a new team was approaching the reviewing stand. "Here comes the Bulgarian team." They, too, were giving the Nazi salute as they passed, but it was their flag bearer that caused the Berliners to howl with delight. As he came by, he dipped the flag so that its tip trailed in the red cinders, and then with a snappy goose step, he strutted by. While this was being done, Hitler and the king of Bulgaria looked at each other, the glow on their faces apparent to the audience. With a thunderous new round of grand applause and shouts, the crowd displayed their approval for the Bulgarian team's salute.

Immediately behind the Bulgarians came the French, two hundred and fifty strong, dressed in blue jackets, white trousers and blue berets. As they came by the dignitaries, the Frenchmen's arms went out, but it was difficult to judge if it was the Olympic or Nazi salute they gave.

"Damn Frogs," Bloomberg mumbled, "they're hedging their bets."

"Gave an eye for them in the last war," Cornwall snarled as he tapped his black eye patch," but I'll be dammed if I can watch this with what's left." He turned away, his face full of disgust.

"Here come the Brits," somebody yelled. As the two reporters focused back on the parade, the British came on in grand style wearing straw hats. As they neared the reviewing stand, instead of giving an Olympic salute or Nazi gesture, the whole team executed an "eyes right." The nature of this team's act was immediately evident for a tangible sullenness pervaded the audience at this slight to their beloved Fuhrer.

"Steady lads," a voice in the correspondent's section called out, the distinctive twang of a Londoner's accent being quite evident.

"Hearts of oak," Cornwall yelled, then called out, "Three cheers for the Brits, hip hip," which was immediately followed by several "Hoorays," from some reporters in the gallery. Twice more he did this, and each time, a feeble chorus responded. The SS trooper didn't look pleased as he took out a pad and began to write, but Cornwall and Bloomberg didn't care, for they were glad of the British team's bravado.

When the Italian Fascists passed though, they gave the right salute and were warmly greeted by the crowd. Following the Italians was the team from Japan. Although their government had just recently signed a treaty with the Reich, the large Japanese squad only got polite applause from the multitude in the stands. The Turks were next. Once they gave their Olympic salute, they maintained that position all around the stadium's track as the audience cheered wildly.

It was then that the next to the last squad came out, preceded by their banner that was, in German, *The Vereinigten Staaten*. The Americans were lead by medal winner Alfred Joachim, the gymnastics champion. As the team approached the dignitaries, the crowd quieted noticeably.

"What will they do?" a voice in Cornwall's section asked in anticipation.

"Shh," said another excitedly, "let's watch."

While the Americans, three hundred and eighty members, came towards the reviewing stand, they executed an "eyes right" as they put their straw hats over their hearts. While the team did this, Joachim held the flag up and, in the tradition of the 1908 Olympics when the Americans said, "This flag dips for no earthly king," Joachim didn't dip the flag in salute.

While the Americans passed, Hitler sat stone faced and stared straight ahead.

All of this was instantly noticed by the crowd who immediately gave its disapproval with only a slight applause, ringed with low whistles, and the stamping of feet. The Berliners were not happy over the American's display of ill manners towards their Fuhrer, and neither was Hitler.

"Swine," he snarled just loud enough for Goring to hear.

"Look at the blacks," the Air Marshall responded with equal disgust. "Why there's that Jessie Owens fellow, my Fuhrer."

"The Americans should be ashamed of themselves, letting those animals on their squad," he replied as he glanced towards Owens. "I will never shake hands with any of his kind," and Hitler spat out the next words like an angry child, "even if they win."

"My Fuhrer," it was Goebbels whispering, "now is not the time," and jerked his head, "remember the film cameras."

Hitler sighed deeply and tried to regain his composure while the last of the Americans went by. After they had gone, a new team emerged from mouth of the Marathon Gate. With their entrance, a huge frantic roar erupted from the audience and swelled across the stadium. "Good," Hitler murmured, a broad grin on his face, "good." He turned towards Goebbels, "this is good."

"As planned," the Reich Minister of Propaganda crowed, "as planned, my Fuhrer." Out on the track's red cinders marched the German team, eight abreast, in perfect order. They were clad in white and wore smart yachting caps and while the orchestra struck up "Deutschland Uber Alles," the Americans were forgotten.

As the host nation's team continued its stroll around the track, and after the first song was finished, the "Horst Wessellied" was begun. With this song's opening strains, the Berliners leaped to their feet, as did Hitler. Like a circus ringmaster, he received the team's salute and while he did, the stadium resounded with an ear splitting din. The noise continued the whole time the Nazi team marched around the track until they took their place among the participating nation's teams. Only then did the crowd quiet in anticipation of what was to come next.

After the parade of athletes, a variety of international speakers came next. These men pontificated at the podium and welcomed the World to the 1936 Games, but few in the audience were really paying attention for they were waiting to witness how the Olympic Oath would be administered.

Following the dignitaries' remarks, the flag bearers of the fifty participating nations came forward and formed a semicircle around a raised dais whose front was silhouetted with an eagle of the Third Reich clutching the Olympic rings. After the flag bearers were in position, a man came forward and was recognized by Cornwall and Bloomberg as Rudolf Ismayr, the German weight lifting champion.

"He's going to give the oath," Bloomberg said as he quickly took out his notebook and began to write.

At that point, Ismayr took the Nazi flag in hand and speaking firmly into the microphone, stated, "We," and his voice boomed out over the loudspeakers, "swear that we will take part in the Olympic Games in loyal competition, respecting the regulations which govern them in the true spirit of sportsmanship, for the honor of our country," and he paused, "and for the glory of sport."

"Did you see what that son-of-a-bitch did?" Cornwall muttered as he elbowed Bloomberg hard while five thousand athletes responded affirmatively to Ismayr's presentation of the Olympic oath.

"Yes," Bloomberg snapped, "the bastard held the Nazi flag not the Olympic flag for the oath!" Bloomberg closed his reporter's steno book. "Let's scram before I vomit."

"Right," Cornwall answered, just as the orchestra broke out into Handel's "Hallelujah Chorus." As the two men pushed their way past the SS aide, headed back towards the Marathon Gate, they were prevented from exiting in that direction and were ushered down a different passageway where a small crowd came towards them. In the lead was a stunning woman in a white coat with light meters hanging from her neck. There were a score of film technicians all about her and they all seemed to be in a hurry. The woman was looking intently at the clipboard and talking excitedly to her entourage, but Cornwall recognized her immediately. "Babe," he called out. "Over here."

She looked up.

"Leni," he shouted in a friendly manner, "over here, Babe."

"Why Frank," she yelled back, as she put out her hand in recognition, "I knew you'd be here, somewhere in the stadium."

She was still a striking woman, Cornwall thought as he took her hand, tall, athletic and alluring as ever, but she seemed tougher in appearance now than when he had first met her in the Alps in the early 1920's. She was a young then, a silent movie star in Max Reinhardt's film. They had met when Cornwall had gone to the Alps to regain his health from his war wounds and had become instant friends, but not lovers. Over the years they had kept in touch, but he hadn't spoken to her since Christmas of last year. Her handshake today was firm, typical of a former mountain climber.

"You're leaving?" she asked, suggestively, a bright gleam in her yes.

"Yes, 'fraid so, but your boss is putting on quite a show ringside."

She chose to ignore that remark on Hitler and turned to one of her underlings. "Go on," Leni ordered, "and tell the cameramen to adjust for the fading light."

"Yes, Miss Riefenstahl," the assistant replied.

"Hurry," Leni added nervously as she grabbed a light meter, "quickly now before we lose any more light."

While the assistant took off at a run, with a wave of her hand she motioned to the others to stand off to one side for it was obvious she wanted to speak to Frank without any prying eyes. Seeing that, Bloomberg also drew back some, but stayed close enough to hear. "Really, Frank," she said, "calling me by that nickname," her tone was flirtatious, not harsh, even though her eyes looked hard. "You are still incorrigible."

"Listen, Babe," he crooned in his best style, "I'm too old for this high falutin' stuff." He winked. "How's the picture going?"

"It will be my greatest achievement, for I have been given exclusive rights." She was beaming as she continued, "so what else could a film director ask for."

"It'll be quite a picture," he replied with a shrug, "so what else can I say," and in a deliberate and soft tone continued, "but I don't care much for your leading man."

"Careful," she countered, her voice low as she glanced off towards her staff, "it's not good to speak so."

"Well, somebody's gotta," Cornwall replied as he touched her arm. "The truth is plain enough to see."

"What truth is that Frank?" she replied cautiously.

"Why," and he looked at her in a manner one gives to an old friend, "how Hitler is the new Nero, and he's already selected his scapegoats."

"I don't care for your inference Frank," she said in a cold way that women use when a man has pushed too hard into their private world.

"Well Babe," he replied, "he is, and you and I both know that. That circus up there just proves it. Hitler's better at the old bread and games ploy than Nero ever was, and that's a fact."

If looks could kill, Bloomberg thought, you've gone too far this time Frank Cornwall, but he was not finished talking yet.

"You've sold out for this picture Leni, but you're not the first director to do it."

"Hitler brings us order and glory," she countered, just loud enough for her staff to hear, "and Germany needs a place in the sun," and pulled back from Frank. "The Fuhrer gives us that place," she stated, then looked at her wristwatch, then back at Cornwall. "Remember, Frank, all is image and the world needs good pictures." Her tone was arrogant as she continued. "I have been chosen to give the world the image of the new Germany," as her voice grew louder, "and you should remember that!"

"And do you remember the Jews, Miss Riefenstahl?" Bloomberg interrupted for he could contain himself no longer.

"Who is this?" she howled in distress.

"He is a fellow traveler in this strange land you call the Third Reich," Cornwall replied. "He works for the Associated Press, and he is my good friend and associate, and his name is Jamie T. Bloomberg."

"Bloomberg," she said the name trying to remember and then it came to her. "Are you the same one who wrote the piece on the Nuremberg Laws of 1935?"

"Yes," he answered.

"And the same Bloomberg," she interrogated, "who did the series on the purging of Jews from the Reich's sports teams?"

"The same, Miss Riefenstahl."

"Frank," she shouted as she glared back at her old companion, "how could you?" for she sounded genuinely hurt. "You impose too much on our friendship."

"It's a hard world, Leni, and you're playing with some bad playmates," and he gestured upwards for, just at that moment, a new roar echoed from the stadium. While it rolled down the passageway, the noise drowned out their conversation for a few seconds.

After it ended, but before he could continue, Leni had turned back towards Bloomberg. "I have no quarrel with the Jews," she spouted, "but I am an artist with a story to present," and she looked at her watch again, and then back at Bloomberg and when she spoke, her tone was stern. "These Olympic Games will show all in Germany, it will show all outside of the Reich, what we Aryans stand for. What greater arena than the Olympics to present the world the true nature of Aryan sports, of the triumph of the will, and of the glory the Fuhrer brings to us. That is the message I wish to convey in this film," and she pointed a finger at Bloomberg, "nothing more, nothing less." She turned sharply back to Frank, the disgust in tone evident as she continued, "Well, the light is fading and I have to go," but she didn't put out her hand. "Goodbye, Frank," she said as if were a snarl, then started to move away. As if this was their cue, her retinue followed.

"She's still quite a woman Jamie," Cornwall said as he looked longingly at her.

"A Temptress in a white coat," Jamie replied, "a real she-Devil."

"Well, I'll give the Devil his due, for he sure knows how to stack'em'," and Cornwall laughed. "Now, let's get going. We've got a story to write and who knows, some of the truth about this Olympics might still come out."

"Do you think the World will believe us?" Bloomberg asked.

"Well," Cornwall muttered as they hurried on, "all we can do is fight the good fight as the Bible says."

"Yea," Bloomberg replied, "but it'll be tough."

"Real rugged," Cornwall murmured, "especially after her film comes out."

As they left, neither reporter noticed, standing in the shadows, the figure of a fair skinned SS officer. He had witnessed the whole encounter and was now smiling. Finally, he turned, headed towards Marathon Gate, a gentle purring emanating from deep inside his throat.

Once outside the stadium, the two Americans looked up and saw the blimp *Hindenburg* cruising gracefully above. "What a sight," Cornwall uttered.

"Look at that," Bloomberg countered as he pointed towards the blimp.

"Christ, can you make out the words on that new banner?" Cornwall asked.

"Yes," Bloomberg replied. "'Today, Germany, Tomorrow, the World.'"

"My God," Cornwall exclaimed, "I hope not."

"Let's get outta here." Bloomberg replied softly. "I've had enough."

As they walked along, a strong breeze had picked up. Its briskness made the Americans shiver, but neither spoke of this sensation. They just tried to endure it and hoped it would pass.

Meanwhile, alone in the stadium's upper deck observation room, the blond SS officer watched them. "Soon," it crooned, for it was confident in what its disciple was accomplishing in the Olympic arena of the 1936, "soon."

FOURTEEN

Hitler and Borman were alone in the room except for the German Sheppard called Blondi by Hitler. The animal was a personal gift, one of the few Hitler had ever accepted in his life, but tonight the dog seemed restless. As Hitler rubbed its neck affectionately, Blondi nuzzled in closer, its tail thumping on the floor. "Good dog," he murmured as the animal looked up, "good boy." It was one of the rare living things the Fuhrer showed his humanity to, but only a few, in private Borman knew. As Hitler had remarked earlier in the evening, "Great Men, must act above the masses. We are not made of average stock, Martin, no, we Great Men are not ordinary and to show love is a sign of weakness for love saps our hardness. Strength is what we must have," Hitler's remarked, as his voice trailed off as he patted the dog's head, "even in our private lives.

Tonight was the night before the grand conference of Europe's leaders to be held to resolve the Sudenten crisis and Borman could sense that the Fuhrer needed companionship, for tonight, he was nervous. The dog too seemed to sense Hitler's mood, but right now seemed to just enjoy the genuine affection being given. Despite all the victories Hitler had accumulated since 1932, tomorrow's meeting was the greatest risk he had taken so far in his rule and Borman knew it. "This gamble," he spoke softly as the three of them were together in the Hitler's mountain retreat, "is greater than the Rhineland, my Fuhrer."

"But this is not '36," Hitler responded confidently. "If our bluff had been called by the old Allies, England and France, we would have seen a coup by the Prussian generals in '36, but we control them now, Borman, so they pose us no threat."

Borman nodded.

"The Sudetenland is the key to further conquest in the East, of that, I am certain," Hitler went on as he rubbed the dog's face and whispered, "Fools."

He was thinking of his generals., Borman surmised.

"What timid things they are, not willing to risk all," Hitler remarked as he looked up and over towards Borman. "Asking me to wait another two years to prepare for the coming war." The dog looked up as if it understood, but it obvious to Borman that the animal loved the unconditional affection. "We shall show them," Hitler continued as he patted Blondi with finality, then pushed the dog away. He rose from his chair while Blondi stared at its master in disappointment. Hitler looked down and pointed a finger, "And Mussolini too, hen!"

Blondi barked just once.

"Good dog," Hitler remarked as he put his hand to the dog's side and gently patted the brute. "Now, be good," and his voice was firm, "go lay down."

The Sheppard looked over and seemed to understand, rose, went to its spot, circled twice and lay on the mat. As it looked outside through the large plate glass windows, Blondi put its head down on its legs, but its ears were alert, the hairs on its neck raised in anticipation

"Well, Borman," Hitler said dryly, "so send in Captain Gruber." Before Borman could reply, Hitler went to the windows and looked out at the mountains, their snow capped peaks standing out like massive sentinels. The valley below was deep in shadows now as the clouds gathered overhead. Only a few scattered stars were managing trying to break through the dense cloud layer, while Hitler stood there, waiting, alone.

After a few minutes, Captain Gruber was ushered into the room by Borman. As Hitler turned, Gruber greeted the Fuhrer with a snappy salute and began giving a report on the weather for the next day. "Thickening clouds till morning, Mein Fuhrer," Gruber said as he handed over the meteorological report, "but the front is passing slowly. We expect no precipitation. Tomorrow will be cloudy, but a good day, overall."

"Thank you Captain," Hitler replied as he skimmed over the report. "Is the Honor Guard all set for the Prime Minister's arrival?"

"Yes, all is in readiness, Mein Fuhrer," Gruber replied. "Prime Minister Chamberlain will be properly greeted by your SS Life Guards."

"Good, good," Hitler murmured as he looked up. "We must put on a good show for our honored guests for tomorrow. "Now," Hitler concluded, "for tonight, I do not wish to be disturbed by anyone till morning, and I do mean no one, Captain Gruber."

"It will be done," he yelped back. "Will that be all, Mein Fuhrer?"

Hitler nodded.

"Then," Gruber snapped as he gave the Nazi salute, "good night, Mein Fuhrer."

The leader returned the gesture with a smaller wave of his hand.

Once outside, Borman left Gruber who went directly to the Duty Officer's station down the hall and found the officer at his desk. "The Fuhrer wishes no one to disturb him tonight, Lieutenant."

"Does that include the Italian?" Lieutenant Linz asked, trying not to hide the sneer on his face.

"Yes," Gruber snapped, "even him."

"That will not sit well with El Duce," the Lieutenant replied, "since the great man doesn't like to be kept waiting and has called twice this evening, already."

"Well," Gruber countered as an evil grin came to his face, "El Duce will have to be trained, properly. Inferiors have to know their place, I think."

"As it should be, Herr Captain," Linz replied, the arrogance of his tone being quite evident.

"Indeed. Now," Gruber concluded with a tone of finality, "you have your orders, Lieutenant. Heil Hitler." Like puppets, they gave the Nazi salute.

Linz picked up his phone and spoke firmly into the telephone's mouthpiece. "Lieutenant Linz here. No one is to be admitted tonight. The Fuhrer has gone to bed and wishes to see no one till morning," and paused. "That is correct," he growled, "no one."

That conversation had been well over a half hour ago and now, inside the Fuhrer's chambers, the leader was pacing as Blondi still lay by the balcony's twin doors. Hitler wished for a cigarette. "Just one," his brain screamed, but he had given them up long ago, but when he was under stress, the old nicotine urge would return. "Damn," and the word echoed in the room. Finally, he threw himself into a chair and sputtered, "I must calm down," then gripped the chair's arms and stared out the huge plate glass windows. "Steady," he mumbled, "steady." After a few minutes, he was able to stabilize himself, but he had grown weary from the energy he had expended, so, quite naturally, he closed his eyes and began to doze. It was his dog's heavy breathing that woke him.

As Hitler became conscious, he beheld the vampire who had rolled the Sheppard on its side and was stroking the dog's exposed underbelly. Hitler could see the vampire's whispering in the dog's ear, but couldn't hear what was being said. Hitler could only see that Blondi's tail was wagging.

After awhile, the vampire rose, turned and faced its disciple. "Well, little brother, I am here," it crooned and extended its hands, palms out and waited patiently.

"Your Excellency," Hitler responded as he got up from his chair, took several steps, and dropped to one knee, head bowed. "All is ready," he murmured.

"Rise," the beast answered with a wave of its hand and so Hitler did. "Go on," the vampire continued as it folded its large hands over its chest and calmly spoke, "report."

"Tomorrow, I will face Prime Minister Chamberlain, Lord," Hitler began, "and I will tell Chamberlain what he wants to hear," the Fuhrer continued, the smile on his face broad and bright. "I will promise Chamberlain peace in our time and I will sign the agreement he demands, stating that if they give me the Sudetenland, another European war shall be adverted since this will be my last territorial demand in Europe."

"Will he believe your lie, little brother?" the vampire asked.

"Chamberlain is no fool, Excellency," Hitler replied. "The Prime Minister doesn't trust me, but he thinks that a slip of paper will hold me to my word. He thinks that I am a man of honor, and that I will keep my word." Hitler stifled a laugh. "I will sign the paper Chamberlain wants and I will promise anything, but I shall not honor the agreement, once I grab hold of the Sudetenland as a result of this appeasement."

The vampire nodded.

"Chamberlain fears a European Armageddon from my threats of war if the Sudetenland is not turned over to me," Hitler continued. "Chamberlain thinks I can be controlled once I sign my name to this agreement. The Prime Minister doesn't believe I am depraved and believes I am an honorable man who will keep my word once it has been written down, formally."

"Strange how good men will not accept evil," the beast exclaimed with a laugh, "such foolishness."

"Yes, Excellency, it is," the disciple continued. "Now that I have Austria and soon the Sudetenland, even Mussolini is afraid of my Lieberstrum. He is a weak friend," Hitler said, "but I can still use El Duce. Even though his power is waning on the international stage, he can still be useful."

"Good," the creature replied, "you've remembered what I told you about friends."

"Yes, Lord," the disciple answered, "I have."

The beast went to the French doors and looked out at the mountains, "Go on."

"Once I have the Sudetenland's mountains," Hitler replied, "the Czechs cannot stop us for Slovakia will fall without a shot when my soldiers move in to take possession of the rest of the country. The old Allies of World War I are unwilling to risk a general war in Europe to save the Slovaks, so the Versailles Treaty will be effectively ended by this Munich agreement." His voice sounded triumphant. "England and France wish to believe that this is my last territorial demand and that from now on, I will be satisfied, once the Sudetenland is restored to the Greater Reich."

"Then on to Poland," the beast countered softly.

"Yes," Hitler said in an equally husky tone, "but what of Stalin?"

"I have begun negotiations with him," the creature replied coldly, "and Stalin will get his piece of our Polish sausage, just as the Czarina did once." The vampire's tone was haughty as it continued, "I will dangle a nonaggression pact at Stalin and he will jump at the opportunity to gain his part of Poland without resorting to a war." The vampire turned away from the windows and continued, "Stalin respects only strength and when he sees that the Allies will not stand and defend Czechoslovakia, well— that wily tyrant will side with us."

"He is a hard man, Lord," the disciple replied, "so will the nonaggression pact between our two nations be enough?"

"True," the vampire answered in a mocking tone, "Comrade Stalin knows no God or Satan, but I will snare that so called man of steel. After this Munich agreement, when the time comes," and the beast walked back towards Hitler, "our Russian card will be played and will startle the Old Allies, so remember, time is not your ally," the vampire whispered, "and your syphilis wends its way through your body, Wolf." It came closer to the Fuhrer. "You have your destiny to fulfill, little brother, and that will not be denied to you, as a faithful follower of Satan."

Hitler sighed and his head drooped at the reminder of his mortality for the vampire had not promised the former corporal a long life.

Gently, the beast put one arm on Hitler's shoulder. "You are the first Fuhrer, little brother, but not the last for our master wishes a sacrifice and you are it. Like Moses, hen," and the vampire paused. "The Promised Land will come, but you will not cross over the Jordan to it, Wolf. If God can call for Abraham to sacrifice his son and for Moses to be deprived of entering the Promised Land, cannot Lucifer do the same?" The beast's voice was louder as it strode from its disciple. "Is not Satan just as great as God?"

Hitler made no reply.

"Is Lucifer not worthy to be loved as much as God?" the vampire asked.

"Yes," Hitler answered, his tone hesitant, "but will I have enough time to do all that is asked of me, Lord?"

"Satan has his plan," the beast quipped as it began to circle the room, "and Lucifer does not reveal all, even to me." The vampire sounded angry. "Satan wishes his kingdom to be accepted by his subjects, his loyal Aryans, and you, little brother, are creating Satan's people. It will be you who will destroy God's peoples, so remember this," and some of the anger left the vampire's voice as it looked at Hitler, "do not let the weak, the timid, or the meek turn you from this goal. Let Lucifer's name be held high by you and yours for you will destroy the Jews, the Poles, the Slavs, the Christians, and even the Communists. You have miles to go before you sleep, little brother," and then the vampire came back to Hitler and placed a hand on the disciple's shoulder. "You choose the right path when I first visited you in the Great War and you will choose the proper course again. You will do great things in the coming days, Wolf, and your name will be honored for centuries to come," and then the vampire leaned in and whispered in the leader's ear. "Be of good cheer. Trust," and its voice was sweet as it continued, "all will be given to you as promised in Satan's name, remember that."

"I will," Hitler replied firmly, his confidence renewed, "I will."

Instantly, the beast held Hitler close and, like ballroom dancers, they intertwined. "You have done well," the vampire said gently, "and Chamberlain cannot stop us, so use this conference, create a glorious victory tomorrow and destroy the last vestiges of the old Allies and their Treaty of Versailles. Ready your armies. Remember, Poland is the prize and the Sudetenland is only the tool to obtain Stalin's duplicity."

"So Stalin will sign the Nonaggression Pact next year then, Lord?"

"Yes, for he will lose confidence with the English and the French after our Munich victory tomorrow. He'll take the Polish scraps we offer him in secret for Stalin is a pragmatist and will make the best deal he can since he thinks you can do him no harm until 1942." The vampire let go of Hitler and looked at him fatherly. "Once we demand the Polish Corridor be returned to us next year, Comrade Stalin will let us fight the Poles and will do nothing on our Eastern borders to threaten the safety of the Reich."

"Will the English and French fight when I demand Danzig, Lord?"

"Yes, but they can do nothing practical to stop our assault next year. Geography is on our side, so they and the French will hide behind the Maginot Line and bluster while your tanks strike like lightening into Poland. The Poles will have to fight on two fronts when Stalin stabs them in the back when he honors our nonaggression agreement," and the vampire paused, "but be careful of that man Roosevelt and his kind."

"The Americans, Lord?" Hitler asked. "Are they not too far away to harm us?"

"Yes," the creature quipped, "but they have a wealth of industry and vast resources and the World hasn't corrupted them enough, so they are still dangerous to us."

"But after we attack and take Russia, Lord," Hitler countered, "we too shall have equal resources to make the planet ours, despite the Americans."

"Yes," the vampire replied as it looked sternly at its pupil, "but we want America to come to us. I have agents there, but the work goes slow. We must pace ourselves, little brother. True evil is always patient, so we will snare America, eventually, but we must play them carefully for the next few years. Once we have the European heartland that stretches to the Ural Mountains, we shall be ready to take on America, then," and the beast's voice soared as he moved back from Hitler, "Satan will be restored to his rightful place." The vampire held its arms out wide as it concluded, "and damned be God."

"And damned be God," Hitler repeated as he dropped to one knee, headed bowed, for he knew the meeting was over. In a few moments, he felt a breeze and looked up hesitantly. The French doors were open and the vampire was gone, but Blondi had crossed over and stood nearby, its tailing pounding into Hitler's side. "Good dog," he said as his hand reached out and patted the German Sheppard. "Tomorrow will be a great day," and he stroked the dog again and moved to close the doors. "Now," Hitler said, "let's go to bed," and expected that the dog would come, but Blondi didn't move. Instead, the dog stood there, looking out into the heavy mist. "Here boy," Hitler pleaded, "here."

Blondi barked once, then turned, and reluctantly ran over to Hitler.

Meanwhile, above the clouds, the vampire soared, dipped into the thick mist, then burst forth again above the banks of white, a multitude of stars twinkling above. "Soon," it purred, "soon," and like a ballroom dancer swirled about, humming, "soon."

END OF BOOK I